Also by Jamaica Kincaid

At the Bottom of the River

Annie John

A Small Place

Lucy

The Autobiography of My Mother

My Brother

My Favorite Plant [editor]

My Garden (Book):

Talk Stories

MR. POTTER

MR. POTTER

Jamaica Kincaid

FARRAR, STRAUS AND GIROUX

NEW YORK

Farrar, Straus and Giroux
19 Union Square West, New York 10003

ISBN: 0-374-21494-8
Library of Congress Control Number: 2002100819

Designed by Jonathan D. Lippincott

www.fsgbooks.com

1 3 5 7 9 10 8 6 4 2

For the Nolands,
Kenneth and Paige
—love.

MR. POTTER

And that day, the sun was in its usual place, up above and in the middle of the sky, and it shone in its usual way so harshly bright, making even the shadows pale, making even the shadows seek shelter; that day the sun was in its usual place, up above and in the middle of the sky, but Mr. Potter did not note this, so accustomed was he to this, the sun in its usual place, up above and in the middle of the sky; if the sun had not been in its usual place, that would have made a great big change in Mr. Potter's day, it would have meant rain, however briefly such a thing, rain, might fall, but it would have changed Mr. Potter's day, so used was he to the sun in its usual place, way up above and in the middle of the sky. Mr. Potter breathed in his normal way, his heart was beating in its normal way, up and down underneath the covering of his black skin, up and down underneath his white knitted cotton vest next to his very black skin, up and down underneath his plainly woven white cotton shirt that was on top of the knitted cotton vest which lay next to his skin; so his heart breathed in its normal way. And he put on his trousers and in the pocket of his trousers he placed a white handkerchief; and all this was as normal as the way his heart beat; all this, his putting on his clothes in just that way, as normal as the way his heart beat, the heart beating normally and the clothes reassuring to Mr. Potter and to things beyond Mr. Potter, things that did not know they needed such reassurance.

Walking to Mr. Shoul's garage to begin his day of sitting in Mr. Shoul's car and taking passengers to and fro, to and fro (he was a chauffeur, he did not mind being a chauffeur), Mr. Potter took shelter from the sun by walking through narrow streets and alleys. He saw a dog, her breasts distended and swollen, her stomach distended and swollen, lying in the shade of a tree native to some of the dry vast plains of Africa, but he did not think that this dog, pregnant and weary from carrying her pups, seeking shelter from that sun, was a reflection of any part of him, not even in the smallest way; and Mr. Potter saw a man sitting in his doorway and this man was blind but his ears were most sensitive to the sounds of footsteps coming to-ward him or footsteps going away from him, and when he heard the sounds of feet coming toward him he got ready to beg the owner of the footsteps for money; this man knew the sound of Mr. Potter's footsteps and he had never asked the owner of those footsteps for anything of any kind. And seeing the blind man sitting in the doorway with his beggar's cup, seeing the blind man expelling into the ground a mouthful of the thick, sticky white phlegm that had slowly gathered in his throat, Mr. Potter did not think that any part of him was reflected in this sight before him. Going toward Mr. Shoul's garage, Mr. Potter saw a boy going to school, he saw most of the garments one family owned hanging on a string of wire, being dried in that way. He saw a woman smoking a cigarette, he smelled the stink coming from some gray-colored liquid that lay stagnant in the gutter, he saw some birds sitting on a fence, and none of this reminded him of himself in any way and that was only because everything he saw was so closely bound to him; between him and all that he saw there was no distance of any kind. And so Mr. Potter entered Corn Alley and walked down it and then left it altogether, and Mr. Potter turned onto Nevis Street and he was then at Mr. Shoul's garage. Mr. Shoul was not there and did not need to be. And on the day Mr. Potter met Dr. Weizenger the sun was in its usual place, up above and in the middle of the sky, shining in its usual way, so harsh and bright, and making the shadows pale and making the shadows themselves seek shelter and causing Mr. Potter to make his way to Mr. Shoul's garage through a passage of narrow alleys and shaded backstreets; on such a day Mr. Potter met Dr. Weizenger.

In Mr. Shoul's garage there were three cars and these cars all belonged to Mr. Shoul, but Mr. Shoul himself was not in the garage with his cars. Mr. Shoul was upstairs in his own house above the garage where the three cars were, and Mr. Shoul by then, that is by the time Mr. Potter arrived in the garage where there were the three cars, had eaten eggs and oat porridge and bread that had been buttered and cheese and had drunk cups of Lyons tea and had said unkind things in an unkind way to a woman who washed his family's clothes and then said unkind things in an unkind way to the woman who had just made his breakfast. These two women were in no way related to him, he did not know them at all, they, like Mr. Potter, were the people he had lived among since leaving that place so far away, the Lebanon or Syria, someplace like that, barren and old. And in the Lebanon or Syria, that old, barren place, Mr. Shoul's breakfast would not have been like this, abundant and new (the eggs had been laid just the day before and the entire breakfast was warm and carefully cooked), but Mr. Shoul could adjust to anything and did adjust to everything as it came his way, and many things came his way, good and bad, and he stayed when it was good and left soon after things got bad. But now things were good and Mr. Shoul stayed at his breakfast, for Mr. Potter was in the garage, wiping down the cars, starting with the one he, Mr. Potter, would drive that day, the one he drove every day, and then wiping down the car that his friend Mr. Martin would drive and then wiping down the car Mr. Joseph would drive. Mr. Joseph was not a friend of Mr. Potter's, Mr. Joseph was only an acquaintance.

And on that day Mr. Potter drove Mr. Shoul's car to the jetty to await a large steamer coming from some benighted place in the world, someplace far away where there had been upheavals and displacements and murder and terror. Mr. Potter was not unfamiliar with upheavals and displacements and murder and terror; his very existence in the world in which he lived had been made possible by such things, but he did not dwell on them and he could not dwell on them any more than he could dwell on breathing. And so Mr. Potter met Dr. Weizenger.

And who was Dr. Weizenger? And just who could answer that question accurately, or who could answer that question with any completeness? No one, really, not the same person who could give an accurate account of any single human being on this earth and all that they might be made of. Dr. Weizenger could not give an accurate account of himself, for an accurate account of himself would overwhelm him. But the man named Dr. Weizenger met Mr. Potter on that day, a day like most of Mr. Potter's days: the sun was in the middle of the sky long before midday, and then long after it was midday, so time, as it might be measured by Dr. Weizenger and known to Dr. Weizenger, had a different meaning to Mr. Potter; this was not their first misunderstanding, this was only one of many. Dr. Weizenger was in a new place, but for so many years now Dr. Weizenger was constantly in a new place. For three hundred years he and all that he came from lived in that place once called Czechoslovakia, he and all that he came from lived in its villages, its towns, its cities, its capital, its provinces, and then, without notice, he and all he came from could not live in Czechoslovakia or its environs anymore. And so Dr. Weizenger had been here, there, and everywhere, and now he was in front of Mr. Potter and this would be his final place, his place of rest, which might account for his hatred and lack of sympathy for Mr. Potter (and all who looked like Mr. Potter).

This sentence should begin with Dr. Weizenger emerging, getting off the launch that has brought him from his ship which is lying in the deep part of the harbor, but this is Mr. Potter's life and so Dr. Weizenger must never begin a sentence; I am not making an authorial decision, or a narrative decision, I only say this because it is so true: Mr. Potter's life is his own and no one else should take precedence. And so this sentence, this paragraph, will begin in this way:

When Mr. Potter first saw Dr. Weizenger, Mr. Potter was thinking of a woman, her name was Yvette, who had just died while giving birth to Mr. Potter's first child, a girl named Marigold; this name Marigold was given to the little girl by Yvette's relatives and it had no significance to them whatsoever and it had nothing at all to do with Mr. Potter, he had not had much to do with Yvette in the first place. And when Mr. Potter thought of this woman, Yvette, who had just given birth to his first child with the name of Marigold, he was not thinking of how the world was filled with happiness, he was not thinking of the golden glow that transformed the world when it had first been born, its new light thick with transparency, its wonder, its mystery, its never-to-be-knownness, its frustrations which would lead to anger and how that anger would lead to a blankness and how it was that in such blankness he, Mr. Potter, existed. When Mr. Potter first saw Dr. Weizenger, his very thoughts, the words that came out of his mouth, were "Mr. Shoul sent me" or "Me ah come from Shoul's." And Mr. Potter saw Dr. Weizenger and Dr. Weizenger saw Mr. Potter. And Dr. Weizenger was not thinking of all that he had left behind, not the thousands of years, not the hundreds of years, not even the last moments that

were now something called history, he was not thinking of anything really, not even his own present unhappiness, not even the wound in his stomach caused
by the turmoil of the world bearing down on the soft-
ness beneath the skin covering his belly, causing his
mind to go blank at one moment and then the next
moment to be filled with images of a childhood so
comfortable, and that comfort was an irritation. "Dr.
Weizenger," said Dr. Weizenger, releasing his own
name into the warm air. Potter, said Mr. Potter to no
one but himself. Such a dead man, thought Mr. Potter
to himself when he saw Dr. Weizenger ('E dead, 'e
dead). Such stupidity, thought Dr. Weizenger to himself when he met Mr. Potter, so much ignorance. And
Mr. Potter was ignorant of Dr. Weizenger's ways, for
Mr. Potter could not read, and so when Dr. Weizenger
asked him to remove his bags from all of the other
bags that had been removed from the great big ship
and placed in the launch and which were now just lying on the floor of the jetty, Mr. Potter was still. What
to do? said Mr. Potter, but only to himself, and he
smiled at Dr. Weizenger. The sea, the sea, the sea that
was so vast, so vast, and vast again, lay in front of
them, Mr. Potter and Dr. Weizenger, and for both of
them it held such peril, such dark memories. On Dr.
Weizenger's suitcase were the words "Singapore" and
"Shanghai" and "Sydney," but Mr. Potter could not

read and so did not know what they meant. And on Mr. Potter's face was written "Africa" and "Europe," but Dr. Weizenger had never had to and would never be able (as it turned out) to read the language in which these words were written. And so standing on the jetty and wondering not at the fact that he was alive, but at the fact that something so incomprehensible as Mr. Potter was standing in front of him, and that strange sun which shone without mercy, and was that the same sea, did it have the same name, and had it followed him after taking him to and from the shores of Greece, Singapore, Shanghai, and Sydney (those were only the ports that had taken him in). Dr. Weizenger almost died just then, he almost fell apart like a badly made piece of furniture, the glue not properly applied, but his wife May (and that was her name, May) came and said, "Well!" and she was from England, even better, she was from that thing called the British Empire, and Mr. Potter understood her English and the tone of voice in which she spoke it.

And there was the sea Dr. Weizenger had just left behind, his back was turned to it and there was the sea Mr. Potter had so long ago left behind, and yet each day that sea defined his life over and over again. Mr. Potter's father had been a fisherman and he had died after cursing the sea for disappointing him, and none of Mr. Potter's brothers, ten of them, had become fishermen. For Mr. Potter was afraid of the sea and then he hated the sea, so much water it was, so much nothing, and that nothing was only water. Mr. Potter longed to feel superior to the sea, he longed to feel superior to something that had such power over him. His mother had by then died. And, having lived deep in the middle of Europe for many years (as had all he had come from), Dr. Weizenger found the sea mysterious, so much water it was, so uncontainable, not like a river, not like a lake; and with what cruelty the sea had carried him toward displacement and homelessness, and so standing before Mr. Potter and so standing before the sea (the sea was on his left side and the sea was on his right side and the sea was to the back of him as he faced Mr. Potter), Dr. Weizenger was confused, and then angry, and then silent. And May said, "Well!" And the silence of the sea (for the sea is silent and only its actions elicit sounds: wails, screams, cries; and then comes grief, remorse, despair) and her saying "Well!" and Mr. Potter saying "Eh, eh," to nothing in particular, held everything they had known in a tight grip. And this moment held in a tight grip was special and ordinary: for all moments are special and all moments are ordinary and who can make them so?

And Dr. Weizenger looked up and saw the sun: the sun was in its usual place, up above and in the middle of the sky, and it was shining in its usual way, so harsh, so bright, and Dr. Weizenger could hardly see his shadow, it had shortened so, as if his shadow had taken shelter from the heat of the sun, as if his shadow had been erased by the sun, and he felt so alone, for he did not even have his own reflection to offer him comfort, and Dr. Weizenger looked up again and wondered if the sun would always be so, and hoped it would not always be so, the day so bright, the sun so constant, in its place, the brightness of the light from the sun not impeded by clouds or any other interference, natural or unnatural; he hoped for some other days, days that might match a feeling, dark and gloomy days, hazy with cold mist days, days in which the sun would go in and out of huge banks of black clouds; days that might match the internal landscape, such days would match perfectly the way he would feel for the rest of his life. For Dr. Weizenger had seen days in which the sun did not shine in any way, not in its usual place, up above and in the middle of the sky, not just coming up above the landscape in the morning and not just disappearing on the horizon in the evening; he had seen days that seemed as if thinned-out milk had been used to draw the landscape in swath after swath, as if the person making the sketch of this landscape was in a state of despair and the milkiness that enveloped the atmosphere was not accidental and not deliberate, only just so, just so, all by itself, Dr. Weizenger had thought at the time. And Shanghai and Singapore and Sydney and all the other places Dr. Weizenger had come from or had just passed through, with their smog and fog and air heavy with moisture and the sun not shining with any reliability from day to day, made Dr. Weizenger suspicious of the day he was now in, the day he was now experiencing, the day in which he was meeting Mr. Potter. Dr. Weizenger had come from a place called Prague, but Mr. Potter had never heard of it, and Mr. Potter could not read and so he could not find it on a map; Mr. Potter could easily find a map, for the British Empire was not ashamed to publicize itself, but Mr. Potter could not read, not a map, not anything else.

All turns in the road harbor death, thought Dr. Weizenger; any turn in the road might lead to death, thought Dr. Weizenger; but the roads to death so far had been accompanied by fog. "Radiant" and then "radiance," thought Dr. Weizenger to himself, and he thought this so deeply that he did not know that the words had crossed his mind. But he was standing in the middle of that light coming from that sun that shone from the middle of that sky, so harshly and it was even so, the middle of the day. "Radiance" and then "radiant," thought Dr. Weizenger, only he said these two words to himself in another language, not the English that Mr. Potter could understand but not read; he said these words in a language that Mr. Potter had never heard, and when Mr. Potter heard

Dr. Weizenger speak, he thought to himself that it was as if Dr. Weizenger came from some other form of humanity, people like that—Dr. Weizenger—cannot even speak properly, so said Mr. Potter to himself. And again, "Radiant" and "radiance," thought Dr. Weizenger, the two words now spinning around in his head; he was thinking of how beautiful light of any kind was and how brightness was better than darkness, and how light itself was the cure for the dark, everything he knew had told him so, all the things he had abandoned had told him that the light was the enemy of the dark and all the things he had come to embrace had insisted that only the light was a prescription for the dark. "Radiant, so radiant," said Dr. Weizenger loudly, but only he could hear himself say it; "and all the goodness in the world, and that goodness is small, and all the evil in the world, and that evil is enormous, is transformed by this radiance and the world then becomes, finally, not indifferent to good or evil, for one is embraced and the other is rejected, such is the power of this radiant light." And Dr. Weizenger was saying all this to himself very loudly, so loudly and yet only he could hear himself say it. And Dr. Weizenger looked at Mr. Potter and Mr. Potter thought to himself, Now this man who cannot speak properly is angry with me, now he is pleased with me, now he is both at the same time.

And so Dr. Weizenger looked at Mr. Potter, Mr. Potter standing in the light of the sun, the sun eternally bright, the sun the very definition of light, the sunlight to which all light bowed, light that was itself and also a metaphor for all other aspiring forms of brightness. But the light in which Mr. Potter stood was not radiant, it was only the sun shining down in its usual way, a way familiar to Mr. Potter yet so unfamiliar and then so disappointing to Dr. Weizenger. And so May said, "Well!" and she meant by this that everything was in its place and so everything should then go ahead, proceed, for there were no impediments that her authority could not subdue, and she said "Well!" and "Well!" again. And Dr. Weizenger was thinking how beautiful light of any kind was, light that did not come from a furnace, a real furnace fed by the fuel of coal or human bodies; light, real light, with its opposite being darkness, real darkness, not a metaphor for the darkness from which Mr. Potter and his ancestors had come.

And the bright light, thought Mr. Potter, was far, far too much (but Mr. Potter's thoughts at that time were not separate from him, Mr. Potter's thoughts and himself were one), and he longed for some protection for his eyes, he longed for some protection for his entire being, but there was none that he had ever heard of. And Mr. Potter squeezed his high-set cheekbones and his low-set brows toward each other into that thing called a squint, and he thought such a thing as a squint was unique to him; he did not know that other human beings might respond in that way to the harsh light cast by the sun; and all human beings might respond so, in just that way, to a surge of bright light: a squint might be a universal arrangement of human features in response to a certain kind of assault. How repulsive is this man, thought Dr. Weizenger; how ugly is his face, thought his wife May. "It might rain soon," said Dr. Weizenger; "It will most certainly rain soon," said Mrs. May Weizenger. No rain will come ('E no rain you know), thought Mr. Potter to himself, but his thoughts were then not spoken out loud and his thoughts were then not separated from himself, his thoughts and himself then, were one.

And as Dr. Weizenger stood on the threshold of the house, his house, on the island of Antigua, the sun was shining and his wife, her name: May Weizenger (now it was Weizenger, but before it could have been Smith or Locke, something like that would do), was standing next to him and he wanted to go through the door and so he did, he stepped over the threshold and he remained just as he had been, the same man who had come from Prague and all the things attached to that, his escape from death, his expulsion from his paradise, his journeys to places with those awful names that he had only known on a map, and now to Mr. Potter and the place which had made Mr. Potter what he was and what he would be, and all of it so without importance, Dr. Weizenger had never even seen it on a map, for no mapmaker yet knew of Mr. Potter and where he came from and what had made him. And Mr. Potter went into Dr. Weizenger's house also and opened all the windows and he showed Dr. Weizenger and his wife May how the windows could be made to do that, open and shut, with their bars turned this way and then that, and Dr. Weizenger was surprised at the very scrupulous simplicity of the working of the windows and immediately dismissed that such beauty, the clean and clear motion of windows opening and then being shut, could have anything to do with Mr. Potter and he wished Mr. Potter would just go away, but Mr. Potter knew very well the person who had made the windows, in some roundabout way they were related; Dr. Weizenger could not have known that and Dr. Weizenger just then did not want to know it, and then again, why should he?

But that opening of all the windows by Mr. Potter, why that? Mr. Potter had entered the house and moved about, entering room by room, and opened all the windows; there were twenty windows all in all but the numbers were not of interest to Mr. Potter and Dr. Weizenger was so suffused with sensation that such a number of windows had no meaning to him then (but only just then, at another time this might not be so, but who knew, another time might come again and then again, perhaps not). And Mr. Potter opened the rooms as if he had authority over not the rooms themselves and not the windows themselves, but as if he had authority over the space outside the rooms, the space beyond the windows. The space beyond the windows was the very air itself, empty of things that were made by human hands, but not empty of things that were the product of the human mind: there were trees, shrubs, herbs, and other annoyances of the vegetable kingdom; there were animals and birds and other annoyances of the animal kingdom; there was emptiness waiting to be filled up with what? with what? and with what again? But Mr. Potter, the entity that made up Mr. Potter, was nothing itself, nothing in the sense of something without worth, nothing in the way of a lighted matchstick when it is not needed, so Dr. Weizenger thought, and so too thought the rest of the world, the rest of the world who could have an idea in regard to anything and then launch that idea into the realm of the everyday.

But that opening of all the windows by Mr. Potter made Mr. Potter look out at all the light outside, how it thrilled him ('E ah make me trimble up inside, 'e ah make me feel funny), for it was the light as he had always known it, so bright that it eventually made everything that came in contact with it transparent and then translucent, the light was spread before Mr.

Potter as if it were a sea of water, it covered and yet revealed all that it encompassed; the light was substance itself and the light gave substance to everything else: the trees became the trees but only more so, and the ground in which they anchored themselves remained the ground but only more so, and the sky above revealed more and more of the sky and into the heavens, into eternity, and then returned to the earth; and Mr. Potter thought, for he was lost in the light outside the window (but which window? For it could have been any of the twenty windows), he thought, but his thoughts then are lost now, his mind went blank and he existed not as a man who could cause pain and would cause pain, and not only as a victim of pain and injustice. And he saw the light outside making everything so transparent and then everything becoming translucent and Mr. Potter was happy, he swelled up with it, happiness, and I was not born yet, he had not yet abandoned my mother when I was seven months old in her womb, my mother had not yet taken all his savings, money he kept in the mattress of the bed they shared together, and run away from him; he could not read or write, he could not go to a bank, and my mother had taken all his savings meant for him to one day buy his own motorcar and carry his own passengers, and when she abandoned Mr. Potter and took all his savings, I was then seven months old in her womb. My mother's name was Annie. And be-

20

cause Mr. Potter could neither read nor write, he could not understand himself, he could not make himself known to others, he did not know himself, not that such things would have brought him any amount of happiness. And because Mr. Potter could neither read nor write, he made someone who could do so, who could even love doing so, reading and writing. And as Mr. Potter stood before the window, seeing the world (for it was the world he was seeing) in that special light, in that special way, he did not think to himself, This is Happiness itself, This is as happy as I will ever be, This is as happy as anyone, any human being, will ever be; he did not think that at all, for he was not at that moment separated from himself, he and that particular sentiment and that particular moment were one: he was happy in that light and all the glory of the world could not exist without him.

And Mr. Potter stood before the window (it could have been any of the windows) and just for a moment he paused, and in that moment all of the world was revealed to him and he could see it clearly, the world, that is, the world and all that was in it and all that would be in it, but words just then failed him, for he could not read and he could not write and then he turned around to see Dr. Weizenger and his wife and made a gesture, he flung his arms out and away from his body, he flung his arms open wide and without hurry, as if to say, Here! All this in front of me is mine

and I want to share it with you, let us live in it together, but Mr. Potter could not read and Mr. Potter
could not write and in any case Dr. Weizenger did not
want to share anything with him; Dr. Weizenger, so
recently placed on the very edge of extinction, did not
want to share anything with Mr. Potter, a man so long
alive in a cauldron of terror. "What is your name?"
asked Dr. Weizenger, "What do they call you?" asked
Dr. Weizenger, and just at that moment Mrs. Weizenger, Dr. Weizenger's wife and also his nurse, said
"Zoltan," she was calling out her own husband's name,
"Zoltan," she said, and Dr. Weizenger turned away
from Mr. Potter and looked toward his wife and Mr.
Potter supposed that he saw her, he was looking at
her, he was looking in that direction over there where
she stood, and what was her name, thought Mr. Potter
suddenly, as if it would matter, as if knowing her
name, the one that was not Mrs. Weizenger, would
ever matter to him. And when Dr. Weizenger looked
at his wife (her name was May, that was the name Mr.
Potter wondered about), something passed between
them, words perhaps, a meaningful silence perhaps; it
was words but they spoke in a language that Mr. Potter did not understand, it was English but Mr. Potter
did not understand it, and that exchange between Dr.
Weizenger and his wife ended and he, Dr. Weizenger,
now turned again to Mr. Potter, resuming his interro-
gation, but silently now, he picked up where he had

left off, as if nothing had come between them, not si‑
lence, not its opposite, and Mr. Potter said, "Me name
Potter, Potter me name," and the sound of Mr. Potter's
voice, so full of all that had gone wrong in the world
for almost five hundred years that it could break the
heart of an ordinary stone, meant not a thing to Dr.
Weizenger, for he had been only recently inhabiting
the world as if it were composed only of extinction, as
if it were devoted to his very own extinction. And Dr.
Weizenger was of the mammal species, not reptile or
amphibian or insect or bird, but of the mammals, and
so used to observing, not being observed, and so used
to acting, not being acted upon. And his own extinc‑
tion had almost succeeded and how surprised he was
by this, and how surprised he would remain for the
rest of his life, as if such a thing had never happened
before, as if groups of people, one day intact and
building civilization and dominating heaven and
earth, had not the next found themselves erased
and not even been remembered in a prayer or in a
joke by the rest of humanity; as if groups of people had
not been erased from the beginning of life and human
memory. And the sound of Mr. Potter's voice as he
spoke his own name, giving his own name the charac‑
ter of a caress (or so Dr. Weizenger thought), made Dr.
Weizenger furious, angry, and how he hated Mr. Potter
then, Mr. Potter whom history had made into noth‑
ing, a thing of no spiritual value, nothing had the lux‑

ury of self-love, and Dr. Weizenger could hear it in his voice, "Me name Potter, Potter me name." Those were the words that were spoken, but the sound of Mr. Potter's voice, so full of love for himself, so full of certainty that his name and he were one, made Dr. Weizenger just then want to shut off Mr. Potter's ability to take in oxygen, he wanted to silence Mr. Potter forever, or certainly just now, but all of this murderous rage was distilled into commands: where to place the suitcases, when to come again and carry them for a ride to some destination or other in Mr. Shoul's car. And Mr. Potter and Dr. Weizenger were standing face-to-face and Dr. Weizenger and Mr. Potter were standing opposite each other, and memory, which is to say, history, that frail recollection, that unreliable gathering of all that has happened, did not abandon them: Mr. Potter took off his hat (it was a cap worn by children, schoolboys, in England) and held it in his hand with his head bowed low, his head had come to a rest on his chest, and he looked at the ground in front of him as it lay at his feet, the floor it was and it was made of pitch pine and he did not wonder who made pitch pine and Mr. Potter did not wonder who had made such an idea as pitch pine possible and then turned it into floors and then tables and chairs, and who made anything valuable. Mr. Potter did not think of any of that, his eyes were cast down on the floor (made of pitch pine) and the floor became a relief, for the floor was nothing, just itself, a floor, a man-made barrier against the shifting disorder of the earth; how Mr. Potter loved the floor just then, just at that moment when he was standing in front of Dr. Weizenger and the views and the light just outside the window (or the windows, as it may be) were now behind him. And when Mr. Potter said to Dr. Weizenger his name, he did not long to know of all the Potters that he came from and how it came to be so that he came from them, he did not seek to interrogate the past to give meaning to the present and the future, he only said his name as if he had been asked to state the shape of the earth or the color of the sky, he said his name with the certainty natural to all true things. And as Mr. Potter stood face-to-face with Dr. Weizenger and as Mr. Potter stood before Dr. Weizenger and heard all Dr. Weizenger's commands in regard to the this (the suitcases) and the that (taking Dr. and Mrs. Weizenger here and there), his mind, his conscious thinking, roused itself from the satisfaction of hearing the music of his own voice saying his own name, and now he suddenly disliked the way Dr. Weizenger spoke English, for the English language did not skip off Dr. Weizenger's tongue as if glad to do so, it did not dance out of his mouth calmly, so sure of itself; Dr. Weizenger did not speak the English language as if he, Dr. Weizenger, and the English language were one seamless, inviolable whole: 'E make pappy show o' 'eself, is what Mr. Potter thought when he heard Dr. Weizenger talk then, that time when Dr. Weizenger had just arrived, so new to the new place that was very old to Mr. Potter, so new to the place that Mr. Potter knew very well, inside out or almost so, inside out.

And Mr. Potter left the Weizengers, that is, Dr. Weizenger and his wife May (for that was her name, May); he left their presence, he left their house and walked out to the car, Mr. Shoul's car, for Mr. Potter was not yet driving his own car, and he opened the door and he sat in the driver's seat and he turned the car's key so that the engine would start the car, making it ready for driving, and then he looked over his shoulder, but only figuratively, for he did not really wish to look backward, and to himself he wondered about the people he had just left behind, Dr. Weizenger and his wife who was also his nurse, her name was May, and when wondering about them then, or at any time, the words to come out of his mouth were, "Eh, eh!" and then, "Eh, eh!" a continuing series of those words, those sounds, "Eh, eh!" "Eh, eh!" And when he got into the car, he placed his right foot on that thing called the accelerator (the car he was driving was made in the United States of America) and he went forward out into the small part of the world that was Antigua, and he drove past the cemetery and he drove past many churches through which all the dead passed on their way to the cemetery, and

26

as he drove he could see the great sea of the Caribbean on one side of the road and the great ocean that was the Atlantic on the other and events great or small did not enter his mind, nothing entered his mind, his mind was already filled up with Mr. Potter.

And Mr. Potter turned his back and walked out of the room in which he had been standing with Dr. Weizenger, Zoltan was his name and his wife was named May, and Zoltan and May, that is, Dr. Weizenger and his nurse, were now all alone, and when they were alone they were Zoltan and May and only when they were not alone were they Dr. Weizenger and his nurse Mrs. Weizenger. And May smiled, not to anyone, not to herself, she only smiled, and this was from a habit developed as a child, for when she had been a child her world was grim, she said her parents had been killed sometimes, had abandoned her sometimes, one way or the other she had no parents, and she only felt the loss of the arm posts of such a thing, called a mother and a father, in the first moments of being alone in a new situation, and her husband being with her at that moment, just after Mr. Potter had walked out of the room, did not make enough of a difference: Nurse May, Mrs. Weizenger, was alone. And she said, "Zoltan?" and Dr. Weizenger did not answer and she did not want him to do so. And May looked down at her feet, she wore shoes that were made of a very good leather from the skin of a cow who had been born and raised and then killed with care in the English countryside and how nice the cow's skin now looked after it had been made into something pleasing (a pair of shoes), and into something that offered protection (a pair of shoes), and into something to cause envy (a pair of shoes); a pair of shoes did not come easily to Mr. Potter. And looking down at her feet, her eyes went across the floor and up the thin wall and the wall stopped some distance from the ceiling and May wondered what was the point of that, but it had a good reason, everything in the world had a good reason to back it up, and the room might have swirled and its entire contents spun around, caught up in the violence of a sudden turn in the world's events, and inside that would be May and all her life right up to the moment she met Zoltan, and her life even after she became Mrs. Weizenger.

And Dr. Weizenger heard his name "Zoltan" as his wife now called it out, only he thought she said "Samuel," the name he had been called when he was a boy in Prague, Czechoslovakia, and he remembered the peace of being himself, the peace of being an ordinary human being, in a position to grant the right to exist or the right to make disappear (this would be an insect, children are always allowed to have power over such things), in a position to judge beauty or its opposite (this would be the color of the noonday sky, children everywhere are allowed to have the power to judge such things); and when he had been a boy in a city in that prosperous place called Europe (and Mr. Potter knew the planet Mars as well as he knew the place called Europe), there were streets and in the streets were little houses placed tightly together, intimately, so intimately that this intimacy produced its opposite, and Dr. Weizenger did not know the names of the people who lived next to him. Dr. Weizenger went to a school, and he had a friend, he had many friends but now he could not remember their names, only the shape of their noses and the shape of their mouths and the color of their eyes and those things: the shape of their noses, the shape of their mouths, the color of their eyes was all that was left; everything else receded as if he was on a train (he had been on many trains, leaving to return, leaving, never to return) and it was pulling away from the platform of the train station, pulling away from a place that had been a destination and now was a place of departure. But this place now with Mr. Potter was a stationary place, Mr. Potter and all he came from had made it so, they had been there for centuries, Mr. Potter and all he came from would not go away; the shape of their noses, the shape of their mouths, the color of their eyes would not go away. And Potter, thought Dr. Weizenger, the name of the man who had just driven them to their new destination, was a name so low, named after the service he offered, a potter, a man named after the sweat of his brow, so thought Dr. Weizenger; but "Zoltan," came May's voice, the voice of his nurse, the word that was his name, said by his wife.

And Dr. Weizenger heard his wife's voice and said to himself, Let a minute pass before I make a response to that, and then he said to himself, Let a second pass before I make a response to that. He told himself, silently, that he would allow a pause before he would make a response to this voice coming from this person who was in the same room with him: his entire world as it had been constituted in the past, the past before he came to Antigua, the past that took place before the hurried exit from one place to the next, their names prominent on atlases made after the sixteenth century: Prague, Budapest, Vienna, Berlin, Shanghai; and houses and streets and rivers and quays and boats and embarkments and arrivals and endless days of rain and never-ending days of sunshine, and milk teeming with cream and then none of that, and conversations about the possibility of the end of the world and then days of the world ending again and again, and within the very days themselves were ends, as if the day did not constitute and define a limitation. And his wife said his name again, "Zoltan," she said, but he heard her say "Samuel" and before him he saw the miracle that he had been, Samuel, a boy whose hair was a pleasing color (it was black), a boy whose eyes had been a pleasing color (they were black), a boy whose presence had made his mother and father happy, but just now he could not remember their faces, the faces of his mother and father, he could only remember their presence, he had had them, that thing, a mother and a father, only now they were lost, like a turn in the road (only the road was his own life), or like a horizon (only the horizon was his own life), they had just vanished, as if they had never been there at all, as if they had not given him that name, Samuel, as if he had not been their only child, they had just vanished into darkness, yes darkness! a vast darkness had descended over many things he had known, not a darkness like the night, and not a darkness that was the opposite of the light in which he was now standing, not a darkness that was the opposite of the light into which Mr. Potter had temporarily disappeared, more like the darkness from which Mr. Potter and all he came from had originated.

Into the middle of the bright sunlight at midday Mr. Potter drove Mr. Shoul's car, leaving Dr.

Weizenger and his wife behind, and when they were no longer in his sight, when he had come some distance from them (a mile or so and a mile was quite a distance to Mr. Potter) they vanished entirely from his thoughts and he became absorbed by the uneven road; its surface was coarse, the thick coating of asphalt no longer lay smooth like the icing on a cake (or something like that), and the road itself was a series of twists and turns and every inch of this road, every foot, every yard, every mile held a danger of the sudden drop off a precipice, a turn in the road so sharply rounded that it might not be a turn at all, it might be the end of the road itself. And Mr. Potter held the steering wheel in his hands, sometimes even caressing it as if it were something to which he could administer pleasure, and the steering wheel itself, from the look of it, from the feel of it, was meant to recall the hard protective shell that was the back of a turtle, but Mr. Potter only held the steering wheel in his two hands and the feel of it was familiar and then again the feel of it was not familiar and it remained a steering wheel; and the Weizengers with their complications involving the world that was beyond the horizon did not now exist, and he drove along the road almost in a stupor and said nothing to himself and sang nothing to himself and thought nothing to himself. Mr. Potter drove along and nothing crossed his mind and the world was blank and the world remained blank.

Mr. Potter, while driving Mr. Shoul's car, was passing through villages named John Hughes, Urlings, Newfield, Barnes Hill, Seatons, Swetes, Freetown, and each village was an entire history unto itself, each village a mouthful of pain, each village inhabited by individual human beings with stories so similar and stories so different; and Mr. Potter, while driving Mr. Shoul's car through these villages, each with their scene after scene of pain, withheld himself from the world around him; some of these villages were in the Parish of St. Paul, the parish in which he was born on the seventh of January, nineteen hundred and twenty-two, and as he drove through the parish in which he was born he withheld himself from the world around him. And through the village of Bolans he entered the Parish of St. Mary and he left the Parish of St. Mary through the village of Emanuel and he made his way up Market Street to Mr. Shoul's garage. And all that time Mr. Potter withheld himself from the world and so when he entered the world of Mr. Shoul and Mr. Shoul's garage which housed the other three cars, also owned by Mr. Shoul, but not the drivers of those cars, men, were not owned by Mr. Shoul—for Mr. Shoul was not allowed to own men then—Mr. Potter still withheld himself from the world.

Mr. Potter was born on the seventh day of January in nineteen hundred and twenty-two in the village of English Harbour in the Parish of St. Paul. His mother's name was Elfrida Robinson and his father's name was Nathaniel Potter. And Nathaniel was the father of eleven children with eight altogether different mothers and Mr. Potter was the last of Nathaniel's children to be born, so by that time Nathaniel Potter greeted Mr. Potter's arrival in the world not with a feeling of happiness or a feeling of unhappiness, not with resignation or with the impulse to revolt against the burden of having another person who needed support of one kind or another, not even with indifference. Nathaniel Potter withheld himself from the world of Mr. Potter, my father, the man who could not read and write and so made someone who could do both, read and write, and so made someone who would always be in love with that, reading and writing. But Nathaniel was a fisherman and he cast his fishnet on Mondays and Thursdays and he went to check his pots on Tuesdays and Fridays and on Wednesdays he mended his fishnets, on Saturdays he counted all the money he had made for the week just past through selling fish and on Sundays, his wife (for he had a wife, only she was not Mr. Potter's mother) made him a dinner of goat stew. But on Saturdays, when counting the money he had made all week, he could see that the money always remained the same, week after week, year in and year out, the money remained the same, but the number of his children did not remain so, the same.

The open sky, stretching from the little village called English Harbour to way out beyond the horizon, was familiar to Nathaniel Potter, and this sky was a blue unimaginable to people who had never seen it before; the eminence that was the sun, traveling such a vast distance, reaching the village of English Harbour as harshness of light and temperature, if you were overly familiar with it, or as a blessing of light and temperature, if you were not familiar with it at all; the water that made up the ocean (it was the Atlantic) and the water that made up the sea (it was the Caribbean) flowed gently and calmly as if it were a domesticated body of water cast large. But the beautiful sky (and it was beautiful) and the beautiful days (for they were that, beautiful) and the beautiful bodies of water (and they were that, beautiful) and all of the beauty of the sky and all of the beauty of the land and all of the beauty of the water were so much a part of Nathaniel Potter, it was as if he had been asked to consider his hands or his eyes or his feet; his life would be not imaginable without them. So too would his life be unimaginable without that water, that land, that sky.

And there was the world of sky above and light forcefully illuminating and forcefully streaming through the sky and the awe of great bodies of water flowing into each other even as they remained separate, and Nathaniel Potter was a fisherman in that world of sky above and light streaming through the blue sky and the bodies of water below it and he was subject to this world, a small something in the great and big world that answered to nothing and no one. And from the sky would fall sheets of rain for days upon days; and the light streaming down through the sky often became blanket after blanket of heat smothering him; and the great bodies of water, ocean and sea, would become so turbulent that the world became uninhabitable to all who lived in it. And in those days, Nathaniel Potter's life narrowed and grew ugly and all the beauty of the sky and the light and the sea was ugly when seen through his eyes. And in those days Nathaniel Potter was beautiful also: his legs were long and strong and they were of help to him as he rowed his boat; his arms were long and strong and they were of tremendous help to him as he rowed his boat into the very deep waters; his eyes, his nose, his mouth, and his hair, which was the color of copper and had the texture of metal shredded to resemble tangled thread, made him beautiful, so much so that he was really the father of twenty-one children who had different mothers but Nathaniel knew only of eleven of them. And in those days of the beautiful sky and the beautiful light and the beautiful waters with the sky leaking, sometimes leaking light, sometimes leaking water, and the light streaking through the sky, sometimes creating intolerable heat, and the waters of the sea so turbulent, Nathaniel Potter found no fish in his pots and when he cast his net no fish were trapped, and this went on for such a long time. And as he grew old, his life grew harder: he could no longer easily make a joke when faced with misfortune: no fish in his fish pots and fishnet. And the sun was in its rightful place in the sky and the sky itself was blue and the waters were calm on the surface and it was an ordinary day just to look at it, there was no trace of commotion just to look at the landscape, the landscape was so untroubled, as if it had never known the hand of man or the wrath of a god, as if it had never been observed, as if no one had ever claimed to own it and as if its ownership had never been contested; as if it had never known so much as the capriciousness that was within nature itself, a capriciousness that was beyond human understanding.

And on a day such as that: Nathaniel Potter could hear the faint sound of all that had been capricious and had come to make up his life: his children and their mothers, his ancestors from some of the many places that make up Africa and from somewhere in Spain and from somewhere in England and from somewhere in Scotland. And the faint sound of all that he was made of caused him to grow angry, caused him to grow almost happy and curious but then angry again, and the anger welled up in him and he was all alone in the world, the world that refused to bear any trace of the capriciousness of history or the capriciousness of memory, the world that had passed away. But Nathaniel Potter could not so simply come into such a day and into such a landscape, for at that moment his very existence was part of all that surrounded him. The very shape of the earth, for instance: he was part of its mysterious and endless beginnings, he was part of its boundaries; the day, the night, the light from the sun forcing its way through the heavens onto the land on which he stood, all this too was part of what made him. How simple he was then, how without knowledge of harm he was then, how beautiful, how innocent, how perfect.

Nathaniel Potter could not read and he did not make a child who could do so. He made eleven children but he did not make one who could read and so write. He made a fishing boat with his own hands, he made the oars with which to row his fishing boat, he sat under a tree and made himself a fishing net, and while he was doing all those things his life flowed out of him and then flowed back into him again; and there was nothing he could make of himself, for he was happy sometimes and sad sometimes and angry sometimes and helpless sometimes and without hope sometimes and there was nothing he could make of himself. How it rained when he did not want it to do so, how the rain refused to come down when he wished it would do so, how fast the dark that is night fell when he wanted the light of day to last longer and to shine brighter, how harsh, as it falls on his bare head, could something so innocent as the rays of the sun be!

And that boat, how did he come to know the way in which it should be made? When he had been a little boy he had sat next to a man who made boats and watched that man do so. And those oars, how did he come to know the way in which they should be carved? When he sat next to the man who built the boats, Nathaniel watched as he made oars. And that fishing net, how did he come to know the ways of making it and repairing any rent in it? That same man who built the boat and made the oars had been a fisherman also and he knew how to make fish pots and how to make a fishing net, and Nathaniel had sat next to him and watched him do all those things, for Nathaniel then was just a boy and that fisherman was his father. And his father taught him how to do all the things that would eventually shape his life, for Nathaniel became a fisherman also. But his father did not teach him how to make children and his father could not teach him how to make children who could read and write.

And when Nathaniel became a fisherman, that is to say, a man who went out to sea in the deep dark of late night and the thinning dark of early morning to catch fish, he no longer thought of his father or anyone who came before him. His life was his own and it appeared to him, his life, as itself, not like another life, it came to him without a reference to anything and he was only himself and he was made up of nothing else. And if someone came upon him then, he could not give an account of himself, not even one that began with "I was born . . ." for he no longer had an interest in when he came into the world. But he was born in the way that all people are born and he was conceived in the way all people are conceived: no one enters the world in the exact same situation.

Oh, memory so fresh, so not! Oh, memory so reliable, so not! His skin, protecting him from the elements outside, protecting him from the emotions inside! The future unimaginable, the past so impossible! The skin had not yet separated from Nathaniel Potter's flesh and bones! He was still young.

And Nathaniel Potter walked to the edge of the land and stepped into his boat and sailed to the edge of the sea as he knew it and cast his net and gathered all that was caught in it; and found his fish pots and gathered up all that had been caught in them and he returned to the edge of the land where it met the sea and he was disappointed, for he had caught only a few fish; how alone he felt in his disappointment. What is the glory of the world? He was so much a part of the glory of the world and he could not see himself. Naked at all times, no matter what covered his body, that was Nathaniel Potter. The sun fell into the black before him; the moon rose up from the black behind him: and in between was history, all that had happened, and at its end was a man named Nathaniel Potter and who was only that, Nathaniel Potter. And he asked himself . . . What? He asked himself, not a thing; not why did this go in that way and something else in another. He grew too large for his shirt and his pants and then after that he became small again, not the way he had been as a boy, he only shrunk from his large manly self, and then he was the size of a boy, but he was not a boy again. And love could have entered into his existence and love, very much so, should have entered into his existence, for almost no one needed it more, but love did not become part of Nathaniel Potter's existence. So unloved he was, but he did not know it and so he could not miss love, for it had never been part of his very being.

And the world lay not before him and not behind him. He stood on the very ground that made up his world and nothing was lost and nothing was gained and then again everything was lost forever and ever. One day when he went to his fish pots, they were filled with nothing, and on that day he needed them to be filled with fish. And one day when he cast his net, he caught nothing, not even the stray piece of rubbish produced by the land or by the sea. And at first he was filled with a feeling of awe, of wonderment, at the perfection of the emptiness: his fish pots, his fishnet, making up, as they did, his life as he knew it, his life as he could feel it; but his immediate need was for a fish pot full of fish and a fishnet, as it coursed through the seawaters not far from the shore, to ensnare scores of anything living in the shallow waters of the sea. And that one day of fruitlessness, that first day of fish pots and fishnet empty of everything, was repeated again and again; for many days after, Nathaniel Potter found his fish pots and fishnet empty of prey, and this prey was the very thing that sustained his world. And after many days of this particular emptiness, of this particular silence, Nathaniel Potter cursed God. And these were his actions: he cut his fish pots from their anchors, letting them go drifting into the shallow and deep waters of the blue sea, and then, removing his trousers, he caused his bare bottom to face the sky and in an angry cry he asked God to kiss it; and his fishnet yielded nothing, not a single thing was trapped in his fishnet, and this fishnet, each knot in it, each stitch in it, he knew well, for he had made his fishnet himself. And he cursed God, it was not a God with any specific character; the God he cursed had only an all-encompassing character, this God he cursed was capable of boundless amounts of good but all of that goodness had been denied to Nathaniel; and this God was capable of boundless amounts of evil and a great deal of it, an intense amount of it, had rained down on Nathaniel Potter. And at the moment of the empty fish pots and at the moment of the empty fishnet, the boundless goodness of this God, the vast waters of the sea on which he sailed in his boat and its contents which provided him with his life's support, was no longer known to him; and at the moment of the empty fish pots and the empty fishnet he was only certain of the boundless amounts of evil that were attached to this God. And Look! was the very word he said to himself. And he looked and on his left side moving right was the world painted in hues of silver and yellow and red and green and blue and white and purple and orange and permutations of all these; and he looked and on his right side moving toward the left was the world and it too was painted in hues of silver and yellow and red and green and blue and white and purple and orange and permutations of these colors. And he looked again, first to one and then to another; and then again to one and then again to the other. And Look! he said to himself again and then again and again and again, he said this word to himself, Look! And he looked outside himself and he looked within himself and it was all the same. And he looked again, but it was always the same: inside and out, it was always the same. The coldness of all that was real, inside and outside; the long, bleak blankness of all that was real, inside and outside; oh, for a day so brand new, Nathaniel Potter said to himself, for though he could not read and he could not write and did not know that he could make someone who could do that, read and write, his feelings, all bundled up in a mass of confusion, were not too far back from the tip of his tongue. And he looked again into the abyss that was the dawn before day and then into the mystery that was the same day's end and could not find himself and he looked into his empty fish pots and his empty fishnet and felt how indecipherable was the world, how it could not maintain a pattern of regularity, how uncertainty was attached to everything he knew, how rain could fall beyond necessity, how the sun could shine with such ferociousness that his whole world would long for its cessation. And looking up to the heavens, he cursed the divine being who had made this world of the ground beneath his bare feet—he did not wear shoes—the sky above his bare head, the seas whose bounty had so often been withheld from him. The trousers he wore were made of cotton that had been grown in fields not far from the village where he lived and that had then been sent bale on top of bale to England, where in a factory it had been made into yard on top of yard of cloth and sent back to a store that was in a village not far from the one in which he lived and it was there that he bought yards of this cloth and had it made into the garment covering that part of his body. The shirt he wore had the same origin and destination as his trousers, and shirt and trousers clung to his lean frame as if they were another kind of skin, clung to his lean body as if he had been born wearing only them, and in that way even his body was mixed up with the world and he could not extricate himself from it, not at all could he separate himself from the world. Each intake of breath was a deep cry of pain, each sigh was an expression of unbearable sorrow.

And: a curse fell on Nathaniel Potter and this curse took the form of small boils appearing on his arms and then on his legs and then on the rest of his body and then at last covering his face. And the small boils festered and leaked a pus that had a smell like nothing that had ever lived before and all his bodily fluids were turned into the pus that leaked out of him and he no longer cursed at whatever it was that he thought had made him and the world in which he had lived, and he even banished from his mind any thoughts of whatever it was, or whosoever it was, that had made him and the world in which he had lived. And when he died, his body had blackened, as if he had been trapped in the harshest of fires, a fire that from time to time would subside to a dull glow only to burn again fiercely, and each time the fierce burning lasted for an eternity. And he died and his death seemed sudden even though he had been marching toward its inevitability for forty-seven years, he was forty-seven years of age when he died, and his death was a surprise just the way each death is, and his death made all who heard of it and all who knew him pause, stop, and wonder if such a thing could happen to them also, for the living always doubt the reality of death and the dead do not know of doubt, the dead do not know of anything. And Nathaniel Potter died and left many children—he knew of eleven—and when he died he could not read and he could not write, and he had not made any children who could do so. Among the names of his children were Walter and Roderick and Francis and Joseph and David and True-hart and John and Benjamin and Baldwin and Mineu and Nigel, their names taken from the history that has been captured in the written word and also from the history of the spoken word. And Roderick was my father but he could not read or write either, Nathaniel Potter only made Roderick Potter and he was my father but he could not read or write, he only made me and I can read and I am also writing all of this at this very moment; at this very moment I am thinking of Nathaniel Potter and I can place my thoughts about him and all that he was and all that he could have been into words. These are all words, all of them, these words are my own.

And many years after Nathaniel's death and burying, I was standing in the graveyard in St. John's, Antigua, looking for the grave of Mr. Potter, Roderick—the son of Nathaniel Potter. He was my own father, and I could not find it. I consulted the grave master, who was just an ordinary man in charge of such an important department, keeping a record of all who had lived and then died, the inevitability of this, dying, making his work constant and predictable, and when I was speaking to him as he was looking into his large black book, a ledger, he did not loom large and grow in importance, not to me and not to himself; he remained just so, ordinary. He could no longer find the exact spot where Mr. Potter had been buried, but it was registered in his book, it was a day, seventy years after he had been born, and the grave master remembered it because three or four, or six or seven, or nine or eleven people had fought with each other at the burial sight, at the very grave, and they had fought with each other because they thought Mr. Potter, my very own father, should have loved them best, this very same man who had not loved anyone in his life, in his own lifetime, should have loved them, each of them, best, better than he had loved anything else or anyone else in this world. Someone named Emma remembered giving him bread to eat when he was a boy and had been hungry; someone named Jarvis said that he had pulled Mr. Potter out of the way of a boiling pot of oil that had been thrown at Mr. Potter by a woman who loved him too much. One of his daughters said that Mr. Potter had raped her but she had loved him so much that not before the moment she saw his coffin being lowered into the ground could she tell of the violence he had perpetrated against her. On and on went the stories of love and hatred, and that was all the grave master knew of Mr. Potter. And the world and its events swirled beneath his feet and the world and its events swirled above his head and the grave master said, while looking at me but not seeing me at all, that no one could be really known until they were dead, only when you are dead can a person be really known, because when you are dead then you cannot modify your actions, you are in a state of such stillness, the permanent stillness that is death, you cannot reply to accusations, you cannot make a wrong right, you cannot ask forgiveness, you cannot make a counteraction so as to make a wrong seem not to have occurred at all, you make the wrong perfect in the imagination, you make the wrong perfect in actuality. All this he said and then he said, "Eh, eh," and he walked away from me and I followed him not too closely, and he wiped away droplets of glistening moisture that had gathered on his forehead with his hand, and this was not to make himself more comfortable, it had no meaning, this removing of droplets of moisture that had gathered on his forehead. He wore a shirt and trousers, and they were made from cotton, but the source of this particular fabric would not have caused him to think of anything, not a moment's pause, not the time it took to make a pronouncement, not anything at all. And the grave master took me to a worn-down mound of earth, and this mound of earth was overwhelmed by clumps of a deeply rooted grass and an equally deeply rooted white lily that bloomed only at night in July. And the grave master said, "Eh, eh," and again he said, "Eh, eh." And always when he said it, "Eh, eh," his voice was filled with surprise, as if everything that was happening right then was so unexpected, or as if everything happening then was like a memory, only taking place again. He wanted to show me where Mr. Potter was buried, he remembered the day well, such a commotion was made at the grave site: Mr. Potter's children on one side but not speaking to each other; the woman he had lived with for many years on the other side, but she not speaking to his children. And they all hurled insults at each other for they had been left nothing. Mr. Potter had left all of his considerable fortune to a distant relative who lived on another island quite far away. And that distant relative from an island quite far away returned to his home with Mr. Potter's money, but shortly after, he too died, and Mr. Potter's considerable fortune disappeared before the eyes of his children and the woman with whom he had lived and who had so tenderly nursed him in the last few days of his life. So much suffering was attached to Mr. Potter, so much suffering consumed him, so much suffering he left behind.

The grave master led me through the graveyard looking for Mr. Potter's grave and I followed him, but not too closely. A small mound under a mahogany tree might be the place, he said, and then he said no, perhaps it was not too far from that flamboyant tree over there, and there were many flamboyant trees, the graveyard had many of that kind of tree growing in it, and so I could not tell which tree in particular he meant. He remembered the day well, he said, the sun was shining very bright, there was not a cloud in the sky, and I did not say to him that the sun always shone very bright here and there was never a cloud in the sky, and is there something to be found in that, the cloudless day, the sun so bright? But I did not say anything to him, I did not agree, I did not disagree. And he remembered the day, he said, the angry people gathered around the grave, the coffin being lowered and people singing hymns for the dead. He heard them sing, he said; they sang, "When I survey the wondrous cross on which the Prince of Glory died." They sang, "Wh-en I sur-vey/the won-drous cross/ On whi-ch the Pr-ince/of Glo-ry died." And did their voices go astray, I wondered to myself, each leaving the other, bending the melody to suit her purpose and his need. And he said, "Yes!" and he pointed to a mound, an eroded mound, a thinning mound, and he said this is where Mr. Potter was buried, this was where he believed Mr. Potter was buried, and perhaps that is the moment he grew weary of me and wanted to get rid of me, for I had made so many demands, and so he showed me the mound under which Mr. Potter had been buried. And the mound was not bare, it was covered with a wormwood, a plant used by my mother and her friends as the main ingredient in an elixir they drank when they wanted to clean their wombs; it was also covered with a plant I now know as *Trades-cantia albiflora*. And the grave master said, "Did you know Potter?" This is what the grave master asked of me, he said, "Did you know Potter?" And I said, "Mr. Potter was my father, my father's name was Mr. Potter." And when I had said this to the grave master, in the most straightforward way I knew, concerning my relationship to Mr. Potter, his intimate knowledge of my mother and the way he had made me and had contributed to my appearance in the world, I was transported back to how I began again, nine months lying in my mother's stomach, warm and curled up and feeding from her own very physical existence, and I knew nothing of Mr. Potter and my own self. And at seven months in my mother's stomach, I lay coiled up not like something about to strike, not like a thing about to be unleashed, but like something benign and eternal, something for which I do not yet have a name. And I am imagining this and yet it is true, this thing that I now imagine is a fact, is something true, it cannot be denied: I lay in my mother's stomach for nine months, but when I had been in my mother's stomach for seven months, my mother, whose name then was Annie Victoria Richardson, left my father, whose name then was Roderick Potter, and this remained his name until his death. And the grave master was not at all interested in my beginnings, for he was concerned only with the well-being of the dead, or at any rate he had only to convince those living that he was a crucial part of their general concern for the dead. And people in the midst of their sorrow and their loss came to him believing that he had never seen such a thing as their sorrow and their loss before, and he did not tell them otherwise and he did not compare so much sorrow and loss here with so much sorrow and despair there. And he asked me, though not speaking to me at all, for he was looking toward the sky or rather toward the heavens, if Mr. Potter was my father ("You Potter pickney?") and when I said "Yes" he did not show me kindness or unkindness, he remained indifferent. And the grave master's name was not Hector or Baldwin, and as I was looking at him, standing near the place where he said Mr. Potter was buried, near the place where he thought Mr. Potter was buried, near the place where, because he had become tired of me, he insisted Mr. Potter was buried, I thought of Mr. Potter for he was my father. And Mr. Potter, like his father Nathaniel, could not read and neither of them could write, and their worlds, the one in which they lived and the one in which they existed, ceased, and the small, irregular stumble that their existence had made in the vast smoothness that was the turning of the earth on its axis was no more and was not celebrated or even regretted by anyone or anything. And from Mr. Potter I was made, and I can read and write and even love doing so.

And Mr. Potter was not an original man, he was not made from words, his father was Nathaniel and his mother was Elfrida and neither of them could read or write; his beginning was just the way of everyone, as would be his end. He began in a long day and a long night and after nine months he was born and Nathaniel Potter knew nothing of his existence until one day, when he was on his way to the shade of the tree under which he mended his fishnet, he saw a small boy who walked like him and his face looked like his own face and the boy (Roderick was his name, he would become Mr. Potter) was accompanied by a woman and her name was Elfrida. And on seeing Mr. Potter, Nathaniel looked the other way, for this was his son, but not a son he had wanted, he had never wanted any of his sons, he had never wanted any of his children; and on seeing Mr. Potter walking with his mother Elfrida, Nathaniel thought not of the joy in loving someone, or of the contentedness that comes from a kind and sympathetic companion, nor did he even think of the satisfaction to be had on seeing the sun set on a day in which everything he did was full of purpose and was useful and was complete. On seeing Mr. Potter, the young boy who was Roderick, the boy who would become my father, Nathaniel thought of the many snags that he would find in the thread as he mended the small breaches in his fishnet, he thought of the smallness that was his life, the pain of entering into the beginning of each day, the way fortune had denied him its goodness, his fish pots so often insufficiently filled, his past never holding a different future. Who am I? never entered into his thoughts, not even when he saw the young Roderick, the boy who became my father, and Nathaniel could not read and he could not write.

A very long "Oooooohhhhh!!!" sighed Nathaniel Potter just before he died and many times before that and it was his only legacy to all his children and all who would come from them: this sound of helplessness combined with despair: "Oooooohhhhh," they all cried and cry, all who came from Nathaniel Potter. And the months were August through September, December through February, and April to the end of July; and the years were the same and the weeks were the same as the years and then so too were the days and the minutes and Nathaniel was trapped in all of that—years and months and weeks and days and hours and minutes—and then he died, the way all people do, he died, and he left Mr. Potter, his son, and Mr. Potter was my father, my father's name was Roderick Potter.

And the end of Nathaniel's life did not bring a beginning to another life. His life ended in the silence so common to everything and in that way he was extraordinary and in that way he was not. And as he was dying, crazy from pain and misery and not with despair, despair did not enter into it, his whole life did not pass before him, and the faces of his children did not float in the invisible air in front of him and he did not call out any names, not his children's, not his own mother's and father's, not his own name. And he did not curse the day on which he was born, he only cursed the day on which each and every one of his ancestors was born. And if all the diseased efforts of his ancestors could come to a resounding end with his death, what would the world be like then? But it was too late for that, already there existed Mr. Potter, Roderick Nathaniel Potter, and that man, Roderick Nathaniel Potter, was my father.

And Mr. Potter, the man who became my father, the man named Roderick Nathaniel Potter who lived to be seventy years old and who in all that time could not read and did not learn to write, was born on the seventh day in January in nineteen hundred and twenty-two and died on the fourth of June in nineteen hundred and ninety-two. And in those seventy years of his life, he did not wish to be anyone better than himself and he most certainly did not wish to be anyone worse; and in those seventy years, each day held its own peril, and each day's peril was so unbearable and then so ordinary, as if it were breathing, and in this way suffering became normal, and in this way suffering became life itself, and any interruption in this suffering, be it justice and happiness, or more suffering and injustice, was regarded with hostility and anger and disappointment. And at the beginning of his seventy years, how unimaginable such an expanse of time, seventy years, was to Mr. Potter, and at the end of his life, all he had been seemed like a day, whatever that might be, a day.

And it was in the middle of the night when there was no wind and there had been no rain for a long time, it was in the middle of a drought, on the seventh of January in nineteen hundred and twenty-two, that Mr. Potter was born and his mother's name was Elfrida Robinson and he was her only child then and he remained her only child for the rest of her life. And in the middle of that long drought and in the middle of the darkest part of the night is how Mr. Potter came into the world and nothing cared and his appearance in the world did not end the drought, the absence of rain, his appearance did not make the world pause. And why should it, why should it be worth mentioning that the world did not pause when Mr. Potter was born, and the world did not ignore his birth, the world was only indifferent to it: to the world, that is, as it is created by God and the world as it is continually created by human activity. And it was in the small village of English Harbour, in the Parish of St. Paul, on the island that was (and still is) Antigua, that Mr. Potter was born, and as he came out of the womb of his mother, Elfrida Robinson was her name, in a small ball of, first, complacency and then exploding into the startling rashness that is a human being, he cried out, but it was not in sorrow, it was only to expand his small, gelatinous lungs, it was only an instinctive effort, his will then being not known to him. And as he emerged from his mother's womb (her name was Elfrida Robinson) she felt herself as if cast asunder, as if split into many pieces, and each piece flung far away from the other and would not be united again and she wondered who she was and what she came from and struggled to remember her own name, for that might amount to something, her name was Elfrida Robinson, and she remembered her name and it was Elfrida Robinson. And her son, for this collection of tissue, bones, and blood was her son, was not held gently by the midwife, Nurse Eudelle (her name was Sylvia Eudelle and her services of midwifery were available to anyone living in the villages of English Harbour, Falmouth, Old Road, Liberta, Urlings, and John Hughes, for beyond those distances she felt a great haughtiness toward people who might need her, and so refused to travel toward their environs, their vicinity). Mr. Potter when born was held with contempt by the person who received him into the world, the midwife Nurse Sylvia Eudelle, for she had brought so many beings just like him into the world, in the very same way as Mr. Potter had come into the world, and no sign of any kind had appeared to reveal to her a departure from her routine, no hallowed moment had made her see these many arrivals she witnessed in the world with any awe and reverence, these many arrivals to her were not unlike the yield of the fields, the yield of the sea, and yields of every kind are commonplace, and are taken for granted, except when yields of every kind fail to do so—yield.

And the pain she felt rending her body, starting with the wet spot between her legs and ending just below her breastbone and making her entire body seeming to be made up of just this area of her body, and all that pain, so big, so big, producing only this small ball of complacency (it was Mr. Potter), and from all that came Mr. Potter, so startlingly rash and innocent, his gelatinous lungs first closely fitted together and then, through his own efforts, expanding so he could then become part of the thing called living. But looking at that small ball of complacency and rashness and innocence: how she loved him, and not knowing what to do with such a thing, this love, she then named him

Rodney, after the English maritime criminal George Brydges Rodney, a man whose criminal nature and accomplishments had become so distorted in retelling that the victims of his actions had come to revere him. Elfrida Robinson's life at sixteen was already shriveled and pinched, and the great expanse of the life of George Brydges Rodney, the English admiral, the second son of Henry Rodney of Walton-on-Thames, overwhelmed her (for he was in the official realm of history) and seemed distant, for he really was in the official realm of history, and the distance was also familiar and common, and for her son, whose appearance in the world had no real meaning for her, she wanted a name that had no meaning at all to her, and this wanting of no meaning made her choose something different, and so she called him Roderick, not Rodney. There are many people in that part of the world, that small part of the overwhelmingly large world, called Rodney, but not Mr. Potter. Mr. Potter's name was Roderick and that man, Roderick Potter, was my father.

And in the middle of the night, just when Mr. Potter was being born and so had no real name yet, the contents of Nurse Sylvia Eudelle's stomach, there since dinnertime six hours ago, had never settled and it bubbled up like some undiscovered fluid, precious or not, traveling just beneath the earth's surface and it made her irritable and then spontaneously explosive and then treacherously calm. The room in which Mr. Potter was born made up the entire house, and the walls of that room, which was really a house in itself, were not painted and nothing hung on them. And in a corner of that room, which was the house in its entirety, stood an enamel pail full of hot water, though by the time Mr. Potter was born the water was no longer hot but it was not cold completely; and in another corner was a box made of thin wood and in this box were sheets made of white cotton and small gowns made of white cotton and a little bonnet made of white cotton and all these things Elfrida had made for the baby she was carrying in her stomach (she did not know then that it would be Mr. Potter); and behind the box made of thin wood was a rat and the rat was still, perhaps asleep or perhaps only taking a rest on a very busy night for a baby was just to be born; and in another corner, that would be three corners now, was a gathering of dust, and in the fourth corner was a gathering of dust also, and all the corners with their contents were indifferent to Elfrida's cries for she was in such pain, and her cries pierced through the walls of the room, the house it was, and reached all the way up to the dark skies, for the clouds were thick and blocked out the light from the moon, which was full and brimming over with brightness, and the stars, which were agleam and blinding with reflected light, and the night was empty to Elfrida's cries, not even an echo accompanied them. And a loud sound, like a grunt and like a dog's bark, escaped through Nurse Eudelle's lips, and a stench, a stinking smell so powerful it could kill anything, anyone, followed and it enveloped the room, which was all that made up the house, even to the four corners, and it stayed in the room, which was all that made up the house, but it did not leave the house and it did not leave the room, and the cry of Mr. Potter's mother as she gave birth to him, a definition of pain itself, overwhelmed all in its presence, all that came near it, all that might hear of it, all that was in its vicinity, all in reality or all only imagined. And Mr. Potter came into the closed and complete world, the world satisfied beyond satisfaction itself, and to his very existence the world was indifferent, the earth spun in its eternal way, the tides of the sea swelled high and then receded, all the mountains everywhere remained majestic, the hills remained comfortingly modest in relation to the mountains, the rivers everywhere flowed gently sometimes, or sometimes in fits of capricious rage; and over time these changed landscapes define constancy itself, and this landscape can make a people; a people will know who they really are when seeing this landscape. And Mr. Potter was born, and all the world was indifferent to this.

And the midwife, Nurse Sylvia Eudelle, took the newly born Mr. Potter, all naked and protected only by his mother's blood and mucus, and plunged him into the bucket of water that stood in one of the corners of that room, really the house, and the water in the bucket had once been hot, but when Mr. Potter had been plunged into it, just born he was then, the water was not hot and it was not cold; the water was indifferent as to temperature. And after removing his mother's blood and mucus from him, the midwife, Nurse Sylvia Eudelle, wrapped him in a blanket and placed him next to his mother, Elfrida Robinson, who was lying in a bed made up of very clean, so very, very clean, rags, and the mother and her child, Elfrida and Mr. Potter, fell asleep exhausted from their common purpose, bringing Mr. Potter safely into the world, a common purpose but to what end? To no end at all. The thin shrill cry of the newborn lingered, it became an unending echo, in the ears of the midwife, Nurse Sylvia Eudelle's ears, and it made her irritable to see them, the mother and her child, asleep, so innocent of everything, all that had just happened inside the room (that was the house) and that had happened beyond it and in its entirety, so much that even this midwife did not know about and could only suspect, could only sense, as if she were gifted to do this also: sense that there were things in the world other than easing the burden of bringing the despised into it.

And in the first hours of his life outside his mother's womb, the newly born Mr. Potter slept next to his new mother, he was her first child and he would be her only child (she had no children besides him), his head next to her gently beating heart, her breathing so regular, so calm, so perfect, as if she had been made that way by God himself. He slept through all of that night and in the morning he drank milk from his mother's breast. He slept through all that morning and then that noon he drank milk from his mother's breasts, and for the first week of his life he slept and drank milk from his mother's breasts and she, his mother Elfrida Robinson, slept and fed her son milk from her breasts. And at the end of that one week it all ended, the sleeping and then feeding, and it ended with such finality, as if it had never happened at all, as if Mr. Potter had never lain next to his own mother and he, her only son, had drunk milk from her breasts and was made so satisfied by this nourishment that he slept a sweet untroubled sleep, and he slept a sleep like that, untroubled, and such a sleep he would never in his whole life of seventy years experience again. How the innocence of Mr. Potter's existence exhausted his mother, how he lived so instinctively and complacently, as if he were an insect and this was one of his many stages of metamorphosis, how in that one week, the first after he emerged from his mother's womb, the reality of his small being was, with certainty, essential to the intricate vastness of all that had been and all that is and all that would be. But then his mother Elfrida Robinson, in whose womb he had spent nine months, a few days more or less, grew tired of him, lying next to her, feeding from her, and then sleeping next to her, and how she longed to be rid of him. And she got out of her bed and placed him on the floor where she made for him a bed from clean rags, very, very clean rags, a nestlike bed, and she left him alone and went outside and went about in the hot, rainless days, but she could hear him, hear Mr. Potter, crying, sometimes from hunger, sometimes from loneliness, and sometimes her heart broke in two when she heard his cries and sometimes her heart hardened, in imitation of some impregnable mineral. And her breasts became parched, barren of her milky fluids (she had willed them so), and for nourishment she brought Mr. Potter, her only son, the only child she would ever have, some thin arrowroot porridge, or some thin cornmeal porridge, or a porridge made from coarse brown seaweed. And Mr. Potter's mother Elfrida Robinson grew tired of him, of the demands he made on her: he needed food, he needed clothes, for he was growing, he needed love but that was out of the order of things, neither of them knew that he needed love, for what could that be, love, between two people such as they were, a mother and a son and in a situation like that: essential to life but without meaning to them in particular.

And looking at that small boy, for he had become a

boy, a small boy, he crawled on the floor of that small room (the house), he sat up, he walked outside of the room (the house), and then he talked, at first in incomplete sentences and then in complete sentences, and when he needed more clothes, she made them with her own hands, for she knew how to do that, and when he got sick and coughed through the night and the breath coming out of his lungs sounded not like breath at all but like the sound of air coming out of the blacksmith's bellows, she sat up with him all through the night and applied a mixture of camphor and tallow on brown paper to his chest, and made a tea from the leaves of the eucalyptus tree and the leaves of many other shrubs and trees and fed it to him and made him well again. As a small child, Mr. Potter suffered the setbacks so typical to anything living, the many ups and downs, but mainly downs, for he seemed always so pale, so sickly, so often on the verge of death itself, death being as always so unpredictable, so whimsical. And when Mr. Potter was a child, a small boy of five or so, his mother grew tired of him and gave him away to a woman named Mrs. Shepherd, and then she walked into the sea, and walked into it as if in walking she would eventually come to something new, some new place that had no resemblance to what she had known, some new place which would obliterate the memory, no really the actuality, of what she had just known. The sea then just looked as the sea was itself, an enormous body of water, the water itself so present that it overwhelmed everything that was known, everything that she, Elfrida Robinson, could know, and as she walked into it, the sea, its reality was out of her senses, but what could that be, out of her senses, for she understood herself so very well, she understood herself completely, she understood outside herself and she understood inside herself and she even understood the very boundary between herself and some something else so different, something not herself at all. But this element, so new, was not water as Elfrida Robinson could recognize it. This water was thick and blank (it was a form of darkness), black, unorderly, moving without anything and thick with something, but whatever it was thick with held no nourishment, and it was so thick and then so heavy, so overwhelming, as if it could be grace, or a blessing, or something good, anything good, but a name could not be found for it, and it was the very texture and atmosphere and reality of the sea, the sea into which Mr. Potter's mother, Elfrida Robinson, walked when she grew tired of his existence. And Mr. Potter's mother walked into the sea without even so much as despair, she did not have even so much as a sense of hopelessness and then going beyond that, she was made up only of what lay beyond that. See her as a small girl motherless, and see her mother before her motherless and that mother, too, motherless, and on and on reaching back not so much into eternity as into a sentence that would begin with the year fourteen hundred and ninety-two; for eternity is the unimaginable awfulness that makes up the past and the unimaginable peace and pleasure that is to come. And where is Elfrida's father, that man named something Robinson? And where is his father and his father before him and on and on into eternity, the eternity of what has been, not the one that is to come?

Can a human being exist in a wilderness, a world so empty of human feeling: love and justice; a world in which love and even that, justice, only exist from time to time and in small quantities, or unexpectedly, like a wild seedling of some necessary and common food (rice would do, or corn would do, or grain of any kind)? The answer is yes and yes again and the answer is no, not really, not so at all. And on that day Elfrida, Mr. Potter's mother she was then and would always be, walked into the sea, everything was so ordinary and itself, as if ordinariness might not sometimes be worth celebrating, as if ordinariness could never be longed for, as if ordinariness could never be missed, as if ordinariness was all there was and anything else was an interruption: the light from the sun sprawled across the small island lazily now, for it had long ago fiercely driven away every shadow, it had long ago with fierceness penetrated every crevice; the sky in some places was a thin blue, as if it had exhausted being that color, blue, as if it was at the very end of being that color, blue, and in some other places the blue of the sky was so intense, so thick was the sky with that color, blue, as if that color, blue, was only then being made, as if it was so new, as if it had never been seen before, and nothing could replace it and this blue might satisfy every known want; and the trees and vegetables grew, not carelessly and wantonly (they lived mostly in a perpetual drought), with leaves everywhere surrounding flowers and fruit and seed, but grew with a careful sadness, sometimes hovering near the ground, as if reaching up to the sky would be a mistake; and sometimes a single tree would arrange itself in this way, half of it dormant, half not, and the dormant half rested and the growing half grew sparingly; and the land itself, the land over which Elfrida Robinson walked on her way into the sea which would then swallow her up, curved and straightened out, rose up into small hills and then flattened out, and the land was not welcoming and it was not rejecting, not on purpose; it was only the land of a very small island, an island of no account, really, and she was of no account, really, only she was the mother of my father and I know I cannot make myself forget that.

And the dress she wore on that day she walked into the sea was made of blue poplin, and even the very fabric that covered her tormented skin had its own tormented history, the very name, poplin, so innocent even in description, so humble when seen in large bolts, so humble when made into a garment worn by Elfrida in any situation, sitting down or walking toward her death being swallowed up by the sea; and the dress had a white collar made of white chambray and sleeves with cuffs of white chambray, and she crossed her arms across her body, just above her waist and just below her breast, as if she were her own child and needed soothing and encouragement just before a difficult task. She wore no shoes, for she did not have any of her own. Her eyes were closed as she walked along the road; on either side of her were landscapes, brown clay heaving up, brown clay sweeping downward, and her eyes were closed not to shut out a beckoning world, not to shut out a world that might tempt her to love it; her eyes were shut because they were so tired, they had been open for so very long. And the world, satisfied in its ordinariness, moved this way and then that, as usual, and Elfrida Robinson, who was even then Mr. Potter's mother, walked without doubt and without purpose toward the sea.

And she walked from the flat center, which was formed by clay, toward the south and southwest, which was hilly for it had been formed by long-dormant volcanoes, and then she walked north and then toward the northeast, and she passed the Bendals stream, which was near the village of Bendals. But a stream, so often a symbol of the gentleness of life in its slow, calm, steady flow, the tender sound it so humbly makes, its very existence a repudiation of so much that is harsh and violent and frightening in the world as we human beings find it—a stream of water could not come to her attention; a stream anywhere, what was that? And she walked toward the sea, but not toward the sea as it was to be found at English Harbour, or Old Road Bluff, or Willoughby Bay, or Nonsuch Harbour, or Boone's Point, or Wetherell Point, or Five Islands, or Carlisle Bay, or Lignum Vitae Bay, or Dieppe Bay. She walked toward Rat Island, a small formation of rock that in silhouette resembled a rodent exposed to its enemies and vulnerable, and this formation of rock was connected to Antigua by a narrow sliver of land, an isthmus. And many years later, for her life ended in nineteen hundred and twenty-seven or sometime not far from around then, my own mother would take me to Rat Island to teach me to swim and I never learned to do that, and on Good Fridays, after the sad mourning service for a man murdered many years ago, my mother and I went to Rat Island to dig for cockles and search for a pink-colored seaweed; we never found enough of either to make a meal, but even so, each year we went again and again after Good Friday services to Rat Island. Nothing of any use grew there, it harbored families of wild pigs, pigs that had escaped domesticity and had grown ferocious, though they were not dangerous, only frightening if you came upon them unexpectedly. And once, while I stood on the shore watching my mother swim in the waters off Rat Island, she took a deep dive and disappeared from my sight and my sense of loss, loss of her, my mother, was so beyond my own understanding that to this day, just to remember it, places me on the edge of just before falling into nothingness, a blank space that is dark and without borders and will always be so. But it is to this place that Elfrida walked, Rat Island, into the bay there, and the seas took her in, not with love, not with indifference, not with meaning of any kind. And it was at Rat Island that Elfrida Robinson died and it was at Rat Island that I falsely thought my mother had died, but at the time of the incident with my mother, I did not know of Elfrida Robinson, I did not know of Mr. Potter, but he was my father all the same and Elfrida was his mother.

And Elfrida Robinson walked into the sea, as if the sea was life and so was to be joyfully embraced, and the sea swallowed her and then twisted her dry like a piece of old clothing and then ground her into tiny bits and then the tiny bits dissolved and vanished from sight, but only from sight, for they are still there, only they cannot be seen. And the moment she surrendered her life was not the very moment the sea closed over her; that moment had come a long time before. The moment she surrendered her life, the moment that the space between her and the world became vast and unknowable, had occurred long before the very powerful reality of the sea's water had overtaken her. Then there was a silence, but only for her; and then there was a blackness, but only for her; and the world retreated to beyond words and order and beauty and all its opposites, but only for her. And after a short while, no one spoke of her again, her courage (for it was that, courage) became cowardice and then strange, so strange that it must not be repeated, and after a short while no one thought of her again, not her only child, her son, Mr. Potter, not his father Nathaniel and not Nathaniel's other children or his other wives or loves or acquaintances, not anyone, and only I now do so, think of her, and she was Mr. Potter's mother, my father's name was Mr. Potter.

See the motherless Roderick Nathaniel Potter, but he did not know himself to be so, motherless. See him a small boy, vulnerable to all that is hard and without heart, to all that is hard and without love, to all that is hard and without mercy. See him a small boy! Eating his penny loaf with no butter on it, drinking his cup of cocoa with no milk in it, never drinking a cup of milk at all; eating his small amount of rice and fish that came from the bottom of the pot, the part that had burned. See his clothes, his khaki pants, his shirt of chambray, thinned in some parts, shredded in some parts, hang without shape on his poor frame, shrink away from his body as if in terror of touching that coarse, scaly covering that is his skin. See him walk across a yard, the soles of his feet bare, naked, as they meet the immediate, near surface of the earth, and sometimes this near surface is soft mud and sometimes this near surface is hard and dry and stony. See him walk down a narrow lane, carrying a letter in his hands, or a brief message on his lips; see him walk down a narrow lane with a large bundle of something important—food, for instance—balanced carefully (not beautifully, he was not a woman) on his head; see him walk down a narrow lane, with the concerns of Mr. Shepherd and his wife, Mistress Shepherd, on his small boy's shoulders. See the small boy, Roderick Nathaniel Potter, asleep on a bed of old and dirty rags, not old and clean rags like the ones that made up the bed on which he was born. See the small boy, so tired, so hungry, before he falls asleep, just before he falls asleep, and hear the grinding sound from his belly, like an old unoiled saw, its blade put to green wood. See the small boy asleep, in a slumber so deep, and his dreams become so much a reality, so much a world of its own, and this world is sometimes the opposite of the one he knows when awake and sometimes it is just the same, and sometimes he does not miss them and sometimes he does not even remember them afterward. See the small boy asleep in a slumber so deep, seamlessly still, his body seems stilled, but not in death, not in the life of death, his body is stilled yet moving with stillness (for yes, that could be so, moving and stillness at one and the same time; it could be so and it was so), and he breathes in and he breathes out, and his chest moves up and down, gently. See the small boy, he would become Mr. Potter, his name then was Roderick Nathaniel on his birth certificate, his name then was Roderick Potter in his mother's mind, his name then was Drickie to all who met him. See the small boy coming awake in the morning, from the deep slumber that had produced a not at all troubling landscape, a landscape with its up and downs, its good and bad; see the small boy awake in the world of his corner in the kitchen, and when he wipes his eyes, a thick liquid, almost like perspiration but it is not, has, while he was sleeping, oozed out of his eyes and thickened into a thin crust, and collected in the corners of his eyes, the corners of both eyes, and the thick coalesced liquid in the corners of his eyes causes him to see at first dimly and falsely and this makes him angry and he violently scrubs the film from his eyes and all that is before him is clear: he will step out of bed, he will put on his clothes (he has no shoes), he walks away from his sleeping life now, he walks into the world and he is in perfect harmony with himself, for perfect harmony is the province of a good God, or the province of the ordinarily degraded. Mr. Potter, my father, Roderick Nathaniel Potter, was of the ordinarily degraded. And see him now round a corner, not yet in possession of the knowledge of his own misery, never to be in possession of the knowledge that the world has rained down on him injustice upon injustice, cruelty upon cruelty, never to be in possession of the knowledge that though his very being was holy, his existence was a triumph of evil. See him round the corner of the alley, any alley, carrying an object in which he takes pleasure: a stone over which he tripped, and the stone has a funny shape for a stone, or a strange texture for a stone, or he picks up the stone for a reason he will never know; and when carrying the stone, as he rounds the corner of the alley, he is skipping, a sign of playfulness, he is tossing the stone in the air and successfully catching it, a sign of playfulness, and he is alone and the joy of himself skipping as he throws a stone into the empty air and catches it is his own, it is something he possesses; and in that moment he is in harmony with his joy and is himself, something he possesses. See Mr. Potter, a small boy, his spirit in harmony with his own actions, his actions in harmony with his spirit; see Mr. Potter, boundless and joyful, as he traverses a very small corner of the world, see him in this way when he was a child, for this is so rare in his life, a joyfulness that was without boundaries. See him as a small boy, for he was

Drickie then, he was not Mr. Potter yet, he was not even Roderick, he was Drickie, a small boy, and his mother had walked into the sea, and his father had died after cursing the small share he received of the fruits of the sea, and he was living with people who could not love him, who could not love anything at all, and neither could he, Drickie, who was not yet Mr. Potter.

And Mr. Potter's mother had smelled of onions, that was all he could remember of her, that she smelled of onions and that the last time he saw her she placed him, this small boy, her only child, in the care of Mr. and Mistress Shepherd, and she walked away from him and for a long time after that (what exactly could that be to a small boy?) he thought she might come back and get him, and then he thought she might come back and say something, anything, to him, and then after that he thought, She will come back just to take a glimpse of me, I will see her as she takes a glimpse of me, and then all this was followed by a large blank space of darkness and light, sometimes separated, the darkness and the light, sometimes mingling, the darkness and the light, and this single blank space of only darkness and light—separated or commingled—was where Elfrida Robinson, his mother, stayed. And when he smelled onions, he remembered her, just the smell of onions being cooked or sometimes the smell enclosing the words as they emerged from someone's mouth, or sometimes the smell of onions just in the air when there was no explanation for it at all, as if the smell in the air was a premonition, a sign of some kind. But onions were not food, onions only flavored food, onions were not a staff of life, onions only made a staff of life more palatable, more enjoyable. And his unfulfilled longing for his mother did not create a feeling of emptiness in him, as far as he knew then, and this did not change up to the day he died; and his mother abandoning him when he was so small and vulnerable to the whole history of evil directed at him and at all who looked like him, and so vulnerable to the many, many small indignities that rained down on him in particular, did not influence his view of the world as far as he knew it then, and this did not change up to the day he died; and after a long time, long after he had been a boy but quite close to the time in which he would die, he could not remember his mother's name, he could not remember his mother's face, the shape of it, the color of it, the feel of it, he could not remember her name, he could only remember that his mother smelled of onions, a food not at all necessary to sustain life. His mother smelled of onions and onions and onions again.

How each moment is brimming over with the possibility of change, how each moment is brimming over with the new; and yet how in each moment the world is seemingly fixed and steadfast and unchanging; how for some of us we are nothing if we are not like the cockle in its shell, the bird in its feathers, the mammal covered with hair and skin; how certain we are that the world will ensure our fixed state of happiness or misery or anything of the vast range in between; how in defeat we see eternity and how so too we see forever and ever and ever again and again in victory; how in some dim and distant way we feel we are nothing and how certain we are that we are everything, all that is to be is present in us and no thing or idea of any kind will replace us.

And there was a man named Mr. Shepherd and he was married to Mrs. Shepherd and they were both descended from African slaves and also other people who were of no real account, to look at Mr. and Mistress Shepherd; they looked mostly as if they were descended from Africans who were slaves. And Mr. Shepherd said . . . but there was nothing for him to say, for everything was in his face, so tautly scrunched up as if mimicking in every way a hand made into a fist, and this fist, powerful for it was a ball of anger made physical, could not release itself and so Mr. Shepherd's face looked like a face, it was a face, but it did not telegraph acceptance, kindness, love, curiosity, or the feeling that what was to come would be a welcome and divinely sanctioned adventure. Mr. Shepherd's face was full of the vigor to be found in the hated. Mr. Shepherd was common, as are all human beings in a way; in a very particular way he was made up of his past, and all human beings, when they find themselves with other human beings, are made up of their past, their past is their true currency. And Mr. Shepherd said nothing even though he spoke many words, but his words could certainly not change the past, nothing could ever do that, the past was a certainty. And Mr. Shepherd paused, he stopped, he froze permanently, eventually, and the world as he came to know it was the taut fist waiting to meet a deserving something, and this was his face. His face was always a representation of these two things: the potential of triumph and the certainty of defeat. It was in such a world and in the care of such two people, Mr. Shepherd and Mistress Shepherd, that Mr. Potter, my father, for Mr. Potter was my father's name, grew up; that is to say, he attached himself to the world, attached himself to the world we all know, the world that is round and has an above and a below and an across, and an over there, and a just right near here and a beyond there and a how could such a thing be: a mystery, something confounding, something that was beyond an explanation on which he could agree. Mr. Potter thickened. And injustice became so real to him it was like breathing, it was like oxygen, it was like standing up, it was like the blue that was the sky, it was like the water that made up the ocean, it was like anything that stood before him: always there, it had a right to be there, and its disappearance would mean a new order, and in that case where would Mr. Potter be? But Mr. Potter kept on, not through his own will, but he kept on growing, that little boy, and Mr. Shepherd hated him as Mr. Shepherd hated his own self and so too he hated all that was around him, but not Mistress Shepherd, he did not hate her, he did not love and he did not hate her, but why? And Mr. Potter grew up into a man, and that man became Mr. Potter, that man that grew up from Drickie, toiling through the perils of life, he was young, new, and foolish, and he survived all of this, the young and the new and the foolish, and then one day he was Mr. Potter and no one had made him that way, one day he knew himself to be Mr. Potter. And Mr. Shepherd taught Drickie how to drive and Drickie—whose name was Mr. Potter eventually, and I came to know him by that name, Mr. Potter, and the name by which I know him is the way he will forever be known, for I am the one who can write the narrative that is his life, the only one really—drove Mr. Shepherd to Shepherd's School, a school for boys like Mr. Potter but those boys did not have a mother who had walked into the sea, and Mr. Shepherd hated the boys of the Shepherd School and he hated Mr. Potter more than that, and he hated himself even more, though he did not know it. And Mr. Shepherd loomed over Drickie in every way that could be imagined, for what else could he do; and the world in its entirety, and in every way imaginable, loomed over Drickie, for that is the way of the world no matter how it constitutes itself, it looms and looms, and Drickie became the opposite of glowing; he grew dull, like something useful made of a precious metal but forgotten on a shelf, he grew dull and ugly, in the way of the forgotten, and this is true: often a thing that is ugly is ugly in itself, and often a thing that is ugly is only a thing that is forgotten, kept from view and kept from memory, and often a thing that is ugly is not only a definition of beauty itself but also renders beauty as something beyond words or beyond any kind of description. And . . .

And Mr. Shepherd acquired a car, a small car in which four people could sit, and he taught Mr. Potter to drive it, and this whole process of learning to drive a motorcar led to many words of abuse from Mr. Shepherd directed at the small boy Drickie, not Mr. Potter yet, but it led to Mr. Potter, for that boy became a chauffeur and he wore a cap and a nice shirt and well-pressed trousers and after he had left his life with Mr. and Mistress Shepherd, he came to call himself Mr. Potter to anyone who wanted to be chauffeured to some destination, and it was all because he had come to have command over that small motorcar. And Mr. Shepherd had acquired his small car from a Mr. Hall, a man whose very physical frame was deformed by the evil events of history, too, settling down on him and then tightening into an inescapable grip, and he knew himself so little that when he spoke his very words seemed an approximation of what he meant to say, and all he meant to say was often false, for Mr. Hall was descended from generations of the triumphant. And when the transaction concerning this car—something they could not make, had no idea how it got made, did not know that their brutal appearance in the new world and their degradation (for the triumphant are just as degraded as the defeated) made this thing, a car, possible—passed between them, how they each felt, though not in equal parts, swelled with importance and pride and how certain they were that most people they met in their everyday life did not receive an amount of divine blessing equal to theirs, for they had motorcars and most people they knew had none. And between them the blessings were not equal: for Mr. Hall then bought a car, brand new, just arrived from England, and it could seat five comfortably and Mr. Shepherd's car was Mr. Hall's old car and it could only seat four. And Mr. Shepherd was more pleased with his first little car, secondhand as it was, that could only seat four, the only car he would ever have, than was Mr. Hall with his brand-new car, his second brand-new car that could seat five.

And that car's secondhandness vanished from Mr. Shepherd's mind, he treasured it so, and if it had been brand new he would not have loved it more, he would not have known how to love it more. Mr. Shepherd had not expected ever to own a motorcar, he had a bicycle, a very good one; even when it became rusty, its rustiness was a part of its very goodness. Mr. Shepherd loved his car so, and this was a new experience, this love, this feeling he had for his small used car that could seat four; for he did not love Mistress Shepherd, he did not love their four children, his four sons, who wanted to be nothing at all but whom Mr. Shepherd knew was meant to dominate a small group of people who were vulnerable in a way Mr. Shepherd had not yet settled on. Mr. Shepherd did not love Mistress Shepherd and he did not love his children, but he knew unwaveringly how important they were to him, like his eyes and his mouth and his heart and his feet, and if he lost any of those things, he would be broken, not heart-broken, just broken, and could not be put back together again in the way he had been before he lost them. And he did love his car and sometimes he would awake himself on purpose just to see how it looked nestled in the deep, deep sea blue that was the color of the night sky, right before midnight; and he loved to see it standing in the rain, its shiny gray permanent coating the color of a skin he could not have imagined, resisting the sudden ferocious downpour, a downpour that had been the object of longing for days, weeks, months, and sometimes even years; he did love his car and wanted to sit in it and be driven

in it, so that the labor of driving the car would not in-
terfere with his love for his car. And Mr. Shepherd
taught Mr. Potter to drive, and in teaching Mr. Potter
to drive, Mr. Shepherd had to reach not too far within
himself to find ugliness and cruelty. He called Mr. Potter stupid, he compared him to invertebrates of every
order, he compared him to the indiscriminately growing members of the vegetable kingdom who were of
no use (as far as Mr. Shepherd knew) and who had
created much nuisance (as far as Mr. Shepherd knew),
and he brought to life the sad specimen that Mr. Potter became (but it was Drickie really, for Mr. Potter
had not been placed in his care). And Mr. Potter took
it all in, cruelty and ugliness, with silence and indifference and as if it were breath itself. And Mr. Shepherd
did not become happy, even as he had been granted
the luxury of expressing his own ugliness without the
slightest retribution; he only became certain of the fu-
tility in everything: a small and private obsession that
might lead to revelation and joy; love itself; the un-
knowableness of who or what made him; the mystery
that he was to himself; the emptiness of spaces and
then their being filled up; the beautifully soft white
Egyptian cotton handkerchief he carried in his pocket
only on Sundays; Mistress Shepherd, his wife, who did
not have to strive to be his wife, she was so simply his
wife, and her general disapproval of her immediate
world and the people who occupied it had a perfec-

tion, like a glass figurine from somewhere far away and completely unfamiliar, somewhere he had read of in a book, and the mere reading of it came to be a personal experience (that would be London). And when Mr. Potter took in Mr. Shepherd's cruelty and ugliness with silence or indifference, all of it—cruelty, ugliness, silence, indifference—became a skin, not like a skin, but a skin; and when his mother Elfrida Robinson walked into the sea after leaving him with Mr. and Mistress Shepherd and he longed for her and then forgot that she had abandoned him to people he did not know and then walked into the sea, the sea which she did not know, all this too became a skin, not like a skin, but a skin itself, a protective covering, something not to be lived without. And Mr. Potter did not know about his father Nathaniel Potter and the voluminous joy he—Nathaniel—experienced from reaping the bounty of the sea, the voluminous joy he took in making so many children, and the lack of sadness or regret that should have come from not loving them really or even caring about their existence, their ups and downs, and all this too, Nathaniel Potter's life and the absence in him of fatherly feelings toward his own children, all of them, became a skin for Mr. Potter, not like a skin, but a skin itself, a protective covering, something that could not be lived without.

And when Mr. Shepherd showed some kindness to Mr. Potter, it was on a Christmas Day (he spent even

Christmas Day in the Shepherds' household), and Mr. Shepherd gave him a small glass of port, a sweet liquor he had purchased from the large general store of Bryson & Sons, and a piece of plum pudding from a tin, purchased in the large general store of Joseph Dew & Sons; and the port would have been awful but Mr. Potter would not have known that, he had no other port with which to make a comparison; and the plum pudding would have been awful, but he could not know that then, he could only know that many years after, when he came to know my mother, Annie Victoria Richardson, and she was a very good maker of many good things to eat but on balance she added to his life an excess of bitterness and ill feeling, so much that he extended it to me, and I can write it down and make clear how all this came to be. And this kindness at Christmas of a glass of port and a slice of plum pudding from a tin did not leave a lasting impression on Mr. Potter, he did not incorporate it into his own life, he did not repeat it in his own household when he eventually had a household; after this Mr. Potter never again drank port; and he was hardly ever kind after that, and when he was kind, it was not at the same time every year and it was not accompanied by anything familiar from a time before.

And this boy in Mr. Shepherd's household, despised for his vulnerability (his mother had abandoned him and had chosen the cold, vast vault that was the sea), held in contempt (for he could not protect himself, he could not protest when he was too tired to do one more thing that was required of him), thought Mr. Shepherd was a man of some distinction and he liked Mr. Shepherd's hat and the way he wore it, as if it topped off something, something substantial, so substantial that no words could be given to it; his hat made Mr. Shepherd, and when Mr. Potter saw Mr. Shepherd, he thought, There is the hat and there is Mr. Shepherd. And Mr. Shepherd had that handkerchief in the pocket of his severely tailored and nicely ironed trousers made of coarse brown linen, and tucked into his trousers was a shirt of white poplin and it was very white, for it took four days to be laundered and two of those days that shirt was spread out in the hot sun on a heap of stones, and was constantly made wet by a woman who did only that, tend Mr. Shepherd's clothes. And Mr. Shepherd's shoes were brown leather and given a proper coat of polish once a week (Sunday evenings) by Mr. Potter and then each evening, by the light of a small oil lamp, Mr. Potter buffed them up. And so Mr. Shepherd went to work each day, to teach and discipline the wayward boys at the Shepherd School, and the boys were so poor and so malnourished they could hardly keep themselves steady, for their stomachs were empty and their clothes were sometimes dirty, sometimes full of holes, and all this made Mr. Shepherd hate them; their misfortune was a curse and to be cursed was deserving of hatred. Mr. Shepherd had been judged cursed and he had been judged deserving of hatred, but when standing before the boys at the Shepherd School, or when standing before Mr. Potter, how could he be expected to remember such a thing? For all people hold so much in common and that is why they despise each other and that is why they show it as soon as they get a chance. Mr. Potter loved the handkerchief in Mr. Shepherd's pocket and he loved the well-ironed pants and the poplin shirt and the beautifully polished shoes (he had been responsible for them all by himself) and these articles of clothing were all he wore himself, with not too dramatic a variation, for his entire life. And Mr. Potter was born in nineteen hundred and twenty-two and he died in nineteen hundred and ninety-two.

And Mr. Potter was born with a line drawn through him, for his father's name did not appear on his certificate of birth and it was always said about him that he had a line drawn through him, and by this it was meant that he had no father, no father's name was written in that column on his birth certificate, only a line had been drawn through it, and that line meant no one was his father; this baby, Mr. Potter, had been born to Elfrida Robinson; she was his mother; he had no father. But when walking with his mother Elfrida one day, his small hand holding on to her big dirty skirt, taking two small slow steps to her one big slow step, they passed by a man sitting under a tree surrounded by fish pots and a fishnet and his mother Elfrida hurled out words at this figure, the man sitting under a tree (it was a tamarind tree, the tamarind tree is native to tropical Asia), and those words were not words of kindness or good wishes or love, and the words came out of his mother's mouth as if her mouth were a weapon and the words ammunition made especially for that weapon, and the words stopped at the back of the head of the man sitting under the tree surrounded by fish pots and a fishnet, and the words must have wounded him for he turned his head, as if to see the source of the pain he felt raining down on him. And Roderick Potter (my father, but he was not that then, he was only a small boy then) saw his own father's face, he did not see the color of the eyes, he did not see the shape of the nose, he did not see the outline of the lips: not how thick they were, not how wide they were, not the shape of the brow, not the shape of the cheeks, not the size of the ears; he saw only the face of that man, that man who was his father and who caused a line to be drawn through him. How well he could remember that face, not the eyes or the nose or the mouth or the ears or the brow or the cheeks, just the face, and he was only two years old then, or only three years old then, or four or five or six or seven years old then, or thirty years then, or fifty years then, or seventy years then—and he was seventy when he died—right before he died then he could see his father's face. That was his father, the man sitting under the tree (it was a tamarind tree) was his father, and no one had told him, he just knew this.

And before this moment of his mother passing the man sitting under the tamarind tree he had never thought of a father and that he did not have one, and at that moment he only knew that man was his father. Looking back, looking over his shoulder then and at three and at four and at five and at seventy years old, just before he died, looking back and just over his shoulder, he could see that face and it was his own face, it was the face he saw when he looked into a mirror, his own face was the face he saw looking back at him from under the tamarind tree or in a mirror. "No use crying over spilled milk" was a saying that he always thought of when thinking of that moment when his mother Elfrida Robinson hurled harsh words at the back of his father Nathaniel Potter and Nathaniel's face was revealed to him and not Elfrida's face, he could not remember what her face looked like. And he did not know where he heard that or why it was said, but only those words collected together into that sentence, "No use crying over spilled milk," came to him as soon as he thought of his father and the first time he saw his father's face. And why was milk spilled, for milk was so valuable, Mr. Potter, when a boy, or in his whole life, had never seen milk spilled, he had never seen so much milk that some of it could be spilled and then spilled in such a way that a saying could be made of it: the milk is spilled, the milk is lost. And Roderick Potter did cry, from the moment he was born until the day he died, but Mr. Potter himself never cried, for no one gave any care to Roderick Potter's cry, everyone told Roderick Potter to stay quiet and sometimes they asked him to do so in a gentle tone of voice and sometimes the tone of the voice was harsh.

A line runs through Mr. Potter's very own self: I hold in my hand a document that certifies the day of his birth, the name of his mother (Elfrida Robinson), the name of the midwife who assisted his mother in bringing him physically into the world, and there is an empty space with a line drawn through it where the name of his father, Nathaniel Potter, ought to have been. And I hold in my hand a document that certifies the day of my own birth (the twenty-fifth of May, nineteen hundred and forty-nine), the name given to me at my own birth (Elaine Cynthia), the name of my mother (Annie Richardson), the place in which she was assisted physically in bringing me into the world (Holberton Hospital), and there is an empty space with a line drawn through it where the name of my father, Roderick Nathaniel Potter, ought to be, for Mr. Potter was my father; my father's name was Roderick Nathaniel Potter. And this line that runs through Mr. Potter and that he then gave to me, I have not given to anyone, I have not ceded to anyone, I have brought it to an end, I have made it stop with me, for I can read and I can now write and I now say, in writing, that this line drawn through the space where the name of the father ought to be has come to an end, and that from Mr. Potter to me, no one after that shall have a line drawn through the space where the name of the father ought to be, and that through him coming through me, everyone after that shall have a father and a mother and so will inherit twofold the great cauldron of misery and small cup of joy that is all of life.

And "A line runs through him" is something I heard my own mother say (her name was Annie Richardson) to someone, a friend of hers I suppose, and I do not now know, which is to say I do not remember, the very first time I heard her say this, but I knew in a way I cannot explain that she was referring to my father, that is, Mr. Potter, and when she said, "A line runs through him," that was not a good thing, I knew she meant that. "A line runs through him," as a curse, that he was a bad man and on top of that he was doomed. I did not know then what made a man doomed and I do not know now, what makes a man doomed. Mr. Potter was born in nineteen hundred and twenty-two and he died in nineteen hundred and ninety-two at seventy years of age. All men are born and then die at some time or another and that would seem to be a natural turn of events, this borning and dying, but when Mr. Potter died his death seemed deserved, his death seemed a punishment, his death was accepted with an impatient gratitude, for a line had been drawn through him and he had no way of erasing it, he did not even know that this line, which passed through him, existed.

And Elfrida Robinson walked into the sea and when Nathaniel Potter died he was separated from all his senses, for he could not see, or hear, or smell, or taste, or feel the earth moving ever so steadfastly underneath his feet. And Mr. Potter was all alone in the world with nothing but a line drawn through him and he stood before nothing, only Mr. Shepherd, the man who had been consigned to oversee his degradation in the world confirmed, and Mr. Shepherd was the headmaster of a school for wayward boys, and all wayward boys have a line drawn through them. And Mr. Shepherd's name was Llewellyn and Mrs. Shepherd's name was Doreen and both their names appeared on the birth certificates of their children, all boys, and their children's names were Horatio and Rodney and John and Francis and when those names failed they were named again Matthew and Mark and Luke and John (this time John was the disciple, not the slave trader), and all those boys, whose parents were named Llewellyn and Doreen and so did not have a line drawn through them, died; and they died sometimes when they had just turned two years of age and sometimes just before turning twelve years of age and sometimes just before they were born. And the wayward boys with the line drawn through them thrived in numbers and as individuals, and they grew up to be wayward men and had children, many children, and all of their children had a line drawn through them. And Mr. Shepherd watched all his children that he, Llewellyn, had with her, Doreen, his wife, die, suffering sometimes before they died, sometimes not suffering at all, dying without even knowing they had lived. And Mr. Shepherd watched all his children, boys born without a line drawn through them, die, and then all the wayward boys who attended the school where he was a headmaster thrived and sometimes they thrived so well that later he would recognize their faces when he saw them across the way; for some of them became occupants of His Majesty's Prison; the Shepherd School was separated from His Majesty's Prison by a walkway made of dirt. And Mr. Potter thrived also in Mr. Shepherd's presence and he grew to be a strong boy and then a strong man and Mr. Shepherd did not like him and did not love him and Mrs. Shepherd never really noticed his existence, not even when she wanted him to run an errand for her, to satisfy a need: her thirst for a cup of water. And Mr. Shepherd passed on to Mr. Potter (he was Drickie then and Mr. Shepherd would never call him Mr. Potter) all that he missed passing on to his dead children, all those boys who never got past twelve years of age, and he passed on to Mr. Potter the love of contempt for all that was vulnerable and weak and in need and lost and in pain, and he passed on to Mr. Potter a love of self and the love of appearing before people well dressed, wearing a nicely pressed and clean pair of trousers, a nicely pressed and clean shirt, a tie, polished shoes, and a cap worn in such a way that everyone who saw Mr. Potter when wearing his cap thought of him as always being in a pleasant mood. And I was weak and vulnerable, not yet even a person, only seven months living in my mother's stomach when Mr. Potter first abandoned me; I was born in nineteen hundred and forty-nine and I never knew his face.

Emerging from Mr. Shepherd's household, not from the fog, or the mist, or the shadow, only emerging from the household of Mr. Shepherd, and emerging at that time when he was no longer a boy but not yet a man, Mr. Potter walked into Mr. Shoul's life, and Mr. Shoul's life, so calmly fragile as is all individual existence, was then vividly engulfed by a sudden fiery collapse of the world as Mr. Shoul knew it. The world as we know it will from time to time do that, collapse, engulfed by a fire generated by a vicious act; the world as we know it will suddenly change its certainties, its very soundness, and will suddenly remind us of fast-moving clouds against a backdrop of an everlasting blue sky, or the firm earth beneath our feet before it turns molten and liquid. Oh, the barren hills that Mr. Shoul could remember were forced to support olive trees and grapevines, and the hills eventually were happy to cease being barren for the olive trees bore much fruit from which came oil and the grapevines bore much fruit from which came wine and vinegar, and the barren hills, now filled with olive trees and grapevines (for this was how Mr. Shoul remembered it), sloped down into a green valley and the green valley was filled with sheep and the sheep had horns and the horns were good and the horns were only good. And Mr. Shoul could see, in his mind's eye (and that would be his memory), himself as a boy walking over hills and valleys (but he never did any such thing as walk a great distance) and at the top of the hills he could reach up and purse his lips and kiss the sky and then walk down into the valleys and the valleys eventually ran into the sea and the sea was not dead, it was only so very still and did not move up and down with waves and wavelets, and when he reached the foot of the valley and was faced with the still sea, just a wave of his hand could make a series of beautiful wavelets all arranged across the stilled waters of the stilled sea (and this too was his memory); and no fish lived beneath and so could not pierce the surface of this stilled sea and no birds hovered just above the surface of this stilled sea. And Mr. Shoul could see, in his mind's eye, himself as a child (he was a little boy) in trousers with short legs and then trousers with long legs, wearing shirts with short sleeves and then shirts with long sleeves; and his skin was the color of the barren hills before they were forced to support olive trees and grapevines, and his arms were arm's length and his legs were just so and his hair was curled naturally.

And not going backward at all, his past not unrolling behind him and with an inward turn of his head can he view it, not that way, not that way at all, but this way, through a sharp glint of light darting out of the corner of one eye (it would be a memory, it would be memory): his father, a thick bolt of flesh himself, surrounded by thick bolts of cloth, silk it was, silk from fabled places (China it was, but China was so far away it seemed a place of many places) and silk of such silkiness that it could only be likened to the petals of roses; and roses now, his mother liked roses, they came sometimes from Damascus, they came all the time from Damascus (but how could that be?), and her arms were plump and dimpled near the elbows and her legs were plump and dimpled near the back of her knees and her cheeks were plump and short hairs grew thickly and formed half a circle just above her eyes and she ate dates and figs which were often piled up in a glass bowl made of pure crystal and placed right in front of her and she looked out of windows and laughed at nothing (but how could he know that, Mr. Shoul then was only a child) and got tangled up in cross words—words that did not dwell in the land of anger, only words that expressed the luxury that is irritation—words that were not really meant for her and got tangled up in malicious acts that were not really directed at her, and all sorts of ancient hatreds that had begun before anyone could even imagine a time that would include her. "Mr. Shoul," said Mr. Potter, but Mr. Shoul could not hear him at all for in his mind's eye he could see his mother and she died while going toward Damascus, not on the road to Damascus itself, just going toward Damascus, perhaps for roses, perhaps for something else, and he could almost hear the last words she said to him before she left, he could almost hear them, but then, not really, not really at all, for he was in his mind's eye and the mind's eye is the land of the almost, the geography of the mind's eye is the almost, its atmosphere is made of the elements, the almost, the as if, the like, the in the vicinity of, the almost, its reality: the almost!

And Mr. Shoul's father continued in his way after his wife died; after his wife died he continued to mingle with the thick bolts of silk that could be likened only to the petals of roses, and the piles of carpets woven from fibers that had been removed from the backs of animals and then dyed with dyes that were so precious and to look at each carpet was to look at some new world that had not been imagined by the person looking at it. Mr. Shoul's father continued in his way after his wife had died, his way of mingling with gold and silver bangles, some by themselves in small velvet boxes, others all mixed up with each other in drawers; and earrings, too, were things he mingled with, and all sorts of other trinkets, none of it essential, none of it necessary. He was a trader and he started out with things that were necessary, pots and pans and cups made of tin and then painted with enamel, and cloth: cotton it was, madras it was, chambray it was, poplin it was, dotted swiss it was, and seersucker. And that was a profitable business, trading in essentials, things that are absolutely necessary; but even more prosperous was trading in things that promised to make life more beautiful, or promised to make life more worthwhile, but of course could do neither, make life beautiful more or less, make life worthwhile more or less. And inside his little trading empire—it was that, a little trading empire—was Mr. Shoul's father, mingling and intermingling with a dazzling array of lights and colors: the red of rubies, the green of emeralds, and the at once cool and hot light of diamonds, the blue of sapphires; all this was in abundance, all this not essential to living, but it is the way of the world to devote itself with a wanton fervor to the things that are not essential; and it does so, always, with the anger of a child who is afraid its will has been too often thwarted.

And then Mr. Shoul's father died also, not on the road to Damascus or the road going toward Damascus, but while crossing the threshold of his dwelling place, his home or trading place; it was all the same, home and place of trading; he dwelled in both, and he died when he was not expected to, for that is the way of death, always so inevitable, always so unexpected, and Mr. Shoul's world was shattered at its center, and this shattering was more like the shattering of the glass bowl made of crystal in which were kept the dates and figs his mother loved to eat and this was because his world was precious to him; but to someone else, someone who did not love Mr. Shoul and did not care to take in his tender existence (he was a human being and so, therefore, his existence was tender and deserved to be protected), his world was shattered as if it were an old bottle and its contents nothing but sediment.

"Eh, eh, Mr. Shoul," Mr. Potter was saying, and it was not really meant to be that Mr. Potter should interrupt the life of the almost, the life of the mind's eye of everyone he meets, any more than it is meant to be that everyone he meets will interrupt again and again his own surprising (to himself, that is) and bewildering (to himself, that is) internal landscape, the view that rests in his mind's eye, the mind's eye being the almost, the as if, the like, the in the vicinity of: the almost. And when Mr. Potter said those words to Mr. Shoul, Mr. Shoul could not hear them for he was in the middle of seeing (almost) and hearing (almost) his world tremble and then shatter irrevocably and he wanted to move away from it all, but there were smells and sounds and there were pictures of things of pleasure, a light snow falling out of that eastern and middle sky, so unexpected was the snow, so miraculous was that snow, so miraculous, but there was no miracle, nothing to save anyone from the many endings that life will present, the ending that was Mr. Shoul's world; it began when he was born and it died when he was all too alive. Who is prepared for that? No one is prepared for that! But just then, just then, when Mr. Potter said, "Eh, eh, Mr. Shoul," to Mr. Shoul, the world in Mr. Shoul's mind's eye (the world of almost) whirled about him like snowflakes (he could remember such a thing), like small bits of uncollected dry rubbish in a yard (Mr. Potter was familiar with such a thing), and Mr. Shoul then entered into his world of the transient, the immigrant, the person without a real home, and he was on ships and the ships were tossed about on the ocean and the seas and when inside the ships he was tossed about, his stomach heaving through his windpipe and up through his nostrils before settling down again the way the ship settled on the ocean and the sea, and then he settled on land and this was in Surinam. But Surinam was not restful; they spoke Dutch there and Dutch seemed so harsh to Mr. Shoul because it was so precise; people always mean what they say, so thought Mr. Shoul, and he didn't like Dutch at all or people who spoke that language, and so he moved on to British Guiana and he didn't like that either, and then he moved over to Trinidad but there were so many people like himself in Trinidad, people from the Lebanon or Damascus, Syria, and they were all selling essential things, like pots and pans and basins and cups made of tin painted with white enamel, and so he moved on, finally coming to Antigua, and there he rested and rested and rested again. He found Mr. Potter and all who looked like Mr. Potter and they were so satisfying, these people who were Mr. Potter and looked like Mr. Potter, that they erased for him the longing for large bolts of silk that could only be compared to petals of roses and the longing to mingle with bangles and bracelets and earrings made of gold or silver and bands of anything studded with precious stones. To win, to capture and so make still, Mr. Potter was everything, everything in the world, everything the world could contain.

"Potter, me ah tell you mahn," said Mr. Shoul, and Mr. Shoul made the sign of the cross over himself, and Mr. Potter did not like to see that, a man making a crossroads of himself, a man making a meeting place for the devil on his own body, making himself a meeting place for his soul to become a bargain, and without a serious look on his face, so thought Mr. Potter when he saw Mr. Shoul making the sign of the cross upon himself, as if he was dividing himself into a crossroads, as if he was offering himself up for a sacrifice and to be made a bargain of at that. And Mr. Potter looked at the ground beneath his feet, the ground in front of him, it was what he always did when the world (and the world was everything he could put his hands on and the world was everything from which he could make nothing) was new and so therefore incomprehensible, or when he understood the world perfectly and yet that understanding led to nothing that he could call happiness, a happiness beyond words; and he looked at the ground beneath his feet and the ground that was in front of him and the ground itself was covered with a thin layer of asphalt that came from a lake containing pitch, not water, in Trinidad and on the ground the shadow of Mr. Shoul was very prominent, so prominent it took up all of Mr. Potter's view. And just then Mr. Potter was thinking to himself, and Mr. Shoul was also thinking to himself, but here is what Mr. Shoul was thinking to himself (for Mr. Potter will always be thinking to himself forever and ever; this is his story):

There was the shadow of Mr. Shoul, this Mr. Shoul who was a boy in the Lebanon whose mother had died on the road heading toward Damascus or the road away from that city, and whose father had died on the threshold of a doorway; there was his shadow lying slanted and flat on the asphalt in full view of Mr. Potter. And Mr. Shoul said, "Potter," and he made the *o* in Mr. Potter's name sound as if the letters *a* and *h* had been joined together and he made the *e* and the *r* in Mr. Potter's name sound like the letters *a* and *h* joined together, and when Mr. Potter first heard his name flying out of Mr. Shoul's mouth he did not recognize himself as he knew himself through his own name, Potter, Mr. Potter, for out of Mr. Shoul's mouth came the word "Patah," not "Potter," and not being able to say Mr. Potter's name in a way that was familiar to Mr. Potter made Mr. Shoul foreign to Mr. Potter.

"Eh, eh, Potter, me ah tell you," said Mr. Shoul, and these seven words served sometimes as a greeting, a welcome, a declaration of affection, a declaration of disapproval of the world in which they both lived, of the world in general, of Mr. Potter and his fellow taxi drivers whom Mr. Shoul employed, of Mr. Potter in particular. And the heat of the sun was harsh from the beginning and the light was harsh also, almost as harsh, to Mr. Shoul, as it had been in Beirut, the Lebanon, or somewhere close by, and Mr. Shoul was no longer a boy, accepting passively the events of the day, natural or artificial; he felt the heat of the sun to be pleasing or not pleasing, however it suited him at any given moment, and he was standing in front of Mr. Potter and his shadow fell between the two of them and his own shadow fell in with Mr. Potter's shadow and in their shadows they were one. And so was Mr. Shoul one with the other drivers of his many cars and their names were Mr. Martin and Mr. Fabian and Mr. Hector, and Mr. Shoul had no real notion of them, except for Mr. Burt, and he liked Mr. Burt for no real reason, not one that he could think of, only that once, when he could not remember the name of that doctor who came from Czechoslovakia—it was Dr. Weizenger—Mr. Burt knew it was Dr. Weizenger; Mr. Burt knew that and only that and he knew nothing more, as far as Mr. Shoul could tell. And Mr. Shoul was one with all the drivers of his many cars but he was only so, one with them, in the shadows. And so, too, in the shadows lay Mr. Potter's mother Elfrida walking into the sea forever and ever and his father Nathaniel cursing God forever and ever, and Mr. Shoul's mother dying on the road to Damascus or the road leading away from Damascus over and over again and his father collapsing into eternity time and again and it would not halt; and they could not speak of it, all these shadows, all these pasts that had been gathered up in the shadows and even then were gathering up in the shadows, for the shadows grew thicker and thicker, and Mr. Potter and Mr. Shoul could never speak of them, their shadows; the world would not allow them to do so, speak of the shadows in which they lived, the world would first shudder and then shatter into a million pieces of something else before it would allow them to do so.

And "Eh, eh, Potter, me ah tell you," said Mr.

Shoul, and at that time his face had been young, but only for a short time (one year), or only for a long time (three hundred and sixty-five days). And Mr. Potter's face itself was indifferent to the passage of time, short or long; and the skin covering Mr. Shoul's face was slack and then bulging thick with blood, and there were many small veins contained in his skin that would reflect accurately his ups and downs, his many travails, even if he did not want them to. And he often did not want them to. And by that time all of Mr. Shoul's memories of youth were mostly held in the flesh that filled up his cheeks and his arms and the middle of his body and his thighs and all these areas of his body, their fullness, could seem to be evidence of prosperity, evidence of Mr. Shoul's prosperity, but his flesh had grown full just at the moments when his life was most turbulent, just when his life was filled with abundance and just when his life was filled with scarcity, and a smile covered Mr. Shoul's face regardless and a smile was a constant, covering his face in its entirety until he met Mr. Potter, and to him Mr. Potter was empty and without importance, which was the exact way he, Mr. Shoul, was feeling about himself. And how the world's turning in its up-and-downness, so dramatic from one thing to the other, and not gradually going from one thing to the other, but one thing and the other were the same, and one thing and the other were complete opposites, and this caused Mr.

Shoul great pain, for he could remember; and how indifferent to the world's turbulence was Mr. Potter for
he too had memory, something so essential to human
existence; but how indifferent to the world's turbulence was Mr. Potter; he could not imagine or know of
his importance to all the turbulence in the world, how
necessary he was to the world of silks and gems and
fields of cotton and fields of sugarcane and displacement and longing for places from which mere people
had been displaced and the flourishing centers of
cities and the peaceable outlay of villages and the disappointments of young women in those peaceable
villages and the anger of young men in those peaceable villages and the screechy tears that flowed first
through the voice and then from the eyes of mothers
living in those peaceable villages and the sinful determination of fathers who lived in those peaceable villages to worship abominable actions. And Mr. Potter
had no inkling of the turbulence: silks, gems, fields of
cotton, fields of sugarcane, and centers of power and
villages that lay in peace because of the violence per-
petuated by those in faraway centers of power.

And on that day, the sun was in its usual place, up and above and in the middle of the sky, and it shone in its usual way, so harshly bright, making even the shadows pale, making even the shadows seek shelter: and that day the sun was in its usual place, up above and in the middle of the sky, but Mr. Potter did not note that, so accustomed was he to this, the sun in its usual place, up above and in the middle of the sky. How young Mr. Potter was then, on that day when the sun was in its usual place, on all those days when the sun was in its usual place, up so high in the sky and shining harshly, making everything it touched wish almost that it had never known light; how young Mr. Potter was then and he walked in a stylish way, pressing the heel down first and then coming forward on the ball of his foot with each step he took as he moved forward and forward to his destination and sometimes his destination was the garage and sometimes his destination was the houses in which the many women he loved lived. Love, love, what was that, and "Me ah wharn you" ("I give you a warning against that") is what Mr. Potter would have said in regard to love and all these many women whom he visited in houses that were made up of one small room and the houses had four windows and two doors and a galvanized tin roof, and when rain fell on this roof it made such a beautiful sound, a music perfect for love or dreaming or singing or thinking or eating or love again, but no rain ever fell, the sun being so always in its usual place. And Mr. Potter was a young man, so young he could make his tightly curled and unruly hair lie flat on his head, and his shirts were always so well washed and ironed by one of the many women living in houses with only one room, and each one of these women was the mother of one of his children and all these children were girls but none of them was me. I was not yet born, my mother was just leaving Dominica after many violent quarrels with her father over the direction her life should take, my mother did not yet know of anyone named Potter and so could have no inkling of me, her firstborn, her only daughter. And Mr. Potter knew many women and he would lie down in a bed with them for brief periods of time, sometimes for an entire night and sometimes he even fell asleep in the same bed with them, and all this would take place in the night, in the dark night, inside the houses with one room where these many different women lived. And these women bore him children, all of them girls, all of them his very own children, his very own issue, and all of them a burden, all of them, these daughters, needing support of one kind or another: food, clothing, and then schoolbooks and above all, his love, and why above all, his love; why include such a thing as love? There they were, appearing before him, one after the other, asking for one thing or the other, appearing before him sometimes at his station just outside Mr. Shoul's garage, sometimes at the jetty as he waited for a passenger disembarking from a trip, and they appeared, their forms wrapped in malice and general ill will, just as Mr. Potter was feeling fully how good it was to be him, Mr. Potter, and not someone else, like Mr. Shoul for instance, or like his friends (Mr.) Martin or (Mr.) Fabian. And who was Mr. Potter in all his full goodness? Who was he? And those daughters of his—and one day I would be among them but at that time he did not even know my mother, Annie Victoria Richardson—those daughters of his with their cries of hunger and illness and ignorance, and their mothers who had words that were like weapons specially forged to make fatal wounds, and their sullying of his good name, for his name was good, his name was Mr. Potter, and accusing him of unfairness and betrayal of his fatherly duties and not being a good person. These daughters had ordinary names just like ordinary people: Jane, Charlotte, Emily, but I was not yet born and so none of these were mine. And these daughters had ordinary names just like ordinary flowers: Rose, Reseda, Lily, Iris, Heather, but I was not yet born and so none of these names were mine. And these daughters had ordinary natures just like ordinary people: mostly good, mostly rotten, mostly without any real interest in the world around them, mostly indifferent to any kindness shown to them, and also cauldrons of malice, mostly incapable of showing kindness to others. And all of these daughters lived with all these mothers in houses that had only one room and four windows and sometimes two doors, and Mr. Potter did not love them, not the daughters and not their mothers, and not the houses in which they lived, or the streets where they lived in the houses, or the villages with the streets and the houses that had only one room. And all these daughters looked like him, they all bore his nose, a broad piece of bone covered with furled flesh lying in the middle of his face, and his nose was itself, just his nose, and could reveal nothing about him, not his temperament, not his inadequacies, not all that made up his character, his moral character, his nose revealed nothing about him, only that all his children, girls, bore his nose, their noses were exact replicas of his.

Oh, the beautiful blue sky above my head, was not something Mr. Potter ever said to himself as he walked to Mr. Shoul's garage in the early morning of a new day as the remains of the last night's dew disappeared into the heated atmosphere; oh, the beautiful blue of the seawater lap-lapping against the shores of Five Islands Bay, hugging the village of Grays Farm, hovering near the open tract that was Greene Bay, a place where people of no account lived, the beautiful blue sea that could be seen from the village of Crab Hill and the village of Freetown and the village of Urlings, that was not something Mr. Potter thought about as he walked to Mr. Shoul's garage. And the fields of sugarcane, stilled now but with their history of horror unspeakable imprisoned in each stray blade, each stray stalk; and so too the fields of cotton and the rows of sweet potatoes and the rows of Irish potatoes and the rows of tomatoes and the rows of carrots and the rows of onions and the rows of pineapples and the rows of things that could be eaten or worn and the rows of things that could cause pain and the rows of things that could alleviate pain: Mr. Potter never thought of all that was before him, all that he passed by, all that he passed by as it was before him. He walked to Mr. Shoul's garage in his shoes made of thin linen and rubber and he wore no socks, and his shirt was nicely ironed and without fault and his pants were nicely ironed with their creases set just where they ought to be, and Mr. Potter walked with that jaunt of his; the way he walked would make anyone observing him think that he did not have a care in the world, and Mr. Potter felt that he did not have a care in the world, certainly not the many little girls with their mothers and each of them living in a house that was only one room with four windows, and how sometimes those little girls were hungry and sometimes those little girls were without clothes and sometimes those little girls and their mothers were on the brink of being turned out of their house which was only one room with four windows. And the dew was vanishing quickly from the presence of the early morning sun, and the dew rose up, forming a picture of thin, worn-out old curtains, shielding a landscape filled up with sea and sky and ships with masts and boats for rowing and canoes and men who will fall overboard, never to be heard from again, and women with trays of fruit on their heads on their way to market, and children who are completely absorbed in the child's world that is made up of powerlessness and pain and the margins of joy, and wet clothes hung on a clothesline, and goats bleating and cows crying as they are milked or just before they are slaughtered, and policemen marching to their station at the governor's house, and the governor just getting out of bed, and the hen laying an egg and the egg being scrambled and then being eaten between two slices of bread and the bread was made by the baker Mr. Daniel, and Mr. Daniel was descended from men and women brought from Africa many years ago and made slaves, and Mr. Daniel, in blissful ignorance, had become a Seventh-Day Adventist. And as Mr. Potter walked toward Mr. Shoul and Mr. Shoul's garage where five cars were waiting for five drivers and Mr. Potter was one of them, small drops of moisture, no bigger than the head of a pin, almost invisible really, gathered in the pit of his arms, in the small crevices of his body, between his toes, on the nape of his neck, behind the lobes of his ear, in the small hidden lines over which the fleshy part of his nose furled, and down his strong calves and down his strong shins and his arms too, and Mr. Potter did not feel uncomfortable; and then a soft breeze blew against his cheek and blew through his entire body and the small drops of moisture evaporated and Mr. Potter did not feel that he had been uncomfortable; and the soft breeze that blew against his body had once been a violent wind which had wreaked so much havoc somewhere far away from the world which Mr. Potter was in just then.

And breeze or no breeze, no wind or wind wreaking havoc on the world, not a thing made Mr. Potter uncomfortable as he walked toward Mr. Shoul and

Mr. Shoul's garage, where, lying quietly and so still as if they could never know movement, were Mr. Shoul's cars. And one of them, the navy blue Hillman with brown leather seats, had so often been assigned to Mr. Potter that it was always referred to as "Potter's car," but it was not Mr. Potter's car, it belonged to Mr. Shoul, this car. And when Mr. Potter sat at the wheel of this car, the navy blue Hillman with brown leather seats, he felt himself one with the car, he felt he possessed the car and that the car possessed him, and the car had no feelings, because a car can never do such a thing, have feelings of any kind, and the car really did belong to Mr. Shoul, and when Mr. Potter felt at one with Mr. Shoul's car, he placed himself with blissful ignorance in Mr. Shoul's possession. "Eh, eh, Potter, me ah tell you" was how Mr. Shoul would greet Mr. Potter as they met so early in the morning in the space that was between the street and the entrance to the garage, and Mr. Shoul greeted Mr. Potter with a warm feeling, a loving feeling, a feeling so expansive and filled up with love that the whole known world could have been healed by it, if only the whole world knew that it needed to be healed by it, this greeting of love and some of its permutations from Mr. Shoul to Mr. Potter. And many years later, many, many years later, when I was about four years old, I saw Mr. Potter standing in the space that was between the street and the entrance to the garage, and that was the first time

I can remember seeing him standing between the street which led to me and the world beyond and the entrance to the garage, which held inside it all the darkness of the world when it has been reduced and made small and powered by evil; and at that time I waved to Mr. Potter, for I could see his face (or I could see what I thought was his face, though I never saw his face at all, not then, not later when he was standing in front of me), and I could see his hat sitting on his head just above his face, and he must have had arms and legs and a body to go with all that, and all of these things that made up Mr. Potter to me, this little girl child of four, who was innocent, all of those things made up Mr. Potter to me and I was in a state of ignorance, for I did not know something that was crucial to understanding my position in the world: when I had seen Mr. Potter, standing between the street and the entrance to Mr. Shoul's garage, I had waved at him, I had stood before him and wished him a good morning, and I had said, through gestures only, that he was mine and I was his, that the world, in all its parts, was complicated, with plates beneath its surface shifting and colliding, with vast subterranean caul-drons of steam and gases mixing and then exploding violently through the earth's crust, that the seemingly invisible spaces between two people who shared a common intimate history were impossible to destroy. And when Mr. Potter saw me wave he did not frown on me, he did not dismiss me with a wave of his hand, he did not curse under his breath my very existence, he only rolled his shoulders, both at the same time, forward and backward, backward and forward, and looked at the spot on the street which I occupied, the street that was filled up with many things, the hustle and bustle of life, the foolish things that make some people's lives laughable and those same foolish things that make some other people's lives a call to death. Not only did he ignore me, he made sure that until the day he died, I did not exist at all. Only waving at him, not crying out of hunger for him, not wanting a roof over my head from him: not anything did I ever come to mean to him, nothing close to his heart did I come to mean to him, and I remember this incident of waving to him because my mother has told me about it and through my mother's words, I have come to see myself waving to Mr. Potter, waving and waving to Mr. Potter as he stood in the space between the openness that was the street and the dark closed space of the garage in which lay all the world of Mr. Shoul, who was from the Lebanon and the areas surrounding that place. And Mr. Potter could not read and he could not write and that time when I stood in the sunlit street waving to him and he refused to see me and then turned and entered the closed dark of Mr. Shoul's garage, I had been sent by my mother to ask him for sixpence to buy a tablet of lined writing paper, for at four years old I could read and I could write but I did not know that Mr. Potter was not capable of doing so, I did not know Mr. Potter at all. I only waved at him and then he turned his back to me. And all this is what my mother has told me and her name was Annie Victoria Richardson and she was born in Mahaut, Dominica, and she is now dead.

And all this my mother has told me, all of this my mother has told me, my entire life as I live it is all my mother has told me. She is now dead, she is dead now. There is a wide undulating plateau filled with yellow grass growing thickly and straight up from the moist dark earth, and the yellow grass grows determinedly beneath a clear blue sky and birds are flying and singing in the morning right after they fall out of sleep and then flying and singing in the evening just before they fall into sleep and their sleep is without trouble and this world of undulating plateau filled with yellow grass and moist earth and blue, blue sky and existence without threat is not the world into which I was born. There is a very large room, it is a house really, and this room is filled up with the treasures of the world, maps and jewels and chairs covered in silk and tables made from the trunks of species of trees that are very hard to find and this room is filled with species of people that are very hard to find and animals that can no longer be found and this room is filled with many things that have been subdued and with people who have been subordinated, and this room is filled with comfort and earthly joy, but I was not born into such a room. I was born in the Holberton Hospital in St. John's, Antigua, on the twenty-fifth of May, nineteen hundred and forty-nine, at five o'clock in the morning. I had by then been in my mother's belly for nine months and I caused her so much discomfort, the nine months I spent in her belly introduced to my mother much pain, a pain she had not known existed or a pain she did not know could exist, and that pain was made up of loving someone whose face was not familiar to her and missing someone whose existence she had not wished for or longed for, and that pain, even as it registered in every part of her body, was also registering somewhere else, somewhere outside her and yet inside her, over there and yet right here, present as if she could touch it, and yet what was it, for it was new and unfamiliar and it came with me, this pain, and the newness of this pain brought a warm feeling and my mother called it love when she could manage it, bear it, and she felt these feelings of pain which she could not control as a violation when she could not manage it, and all of these feelings, love, violation, hatred, came to my mother and they were new to her and I was new to her and as I came into the world on that Wednesday morning at five o'clock so new with that pain, her self, her physical self, being split open, not into two pieces, just her one self being split open, and

I came out of this split and for the rest of her whole life she could not be wholly and only one, just herself, just Annie Victoria Richardson, for the rest of her whole life I stood between her, between this one part that had been split open. And it was through this opening from which I came, this opening that once becoming so could never join up together again, it was because of this opening that an unbridgeable gulf rested between my mother, Annie Victoria Richardson, and myself, and this gulf was not caused by Mr. Potter, Mr. Potter was not central to this gulf, and yet he was an essential element of it, profoundly incidental and so arbitrarily essential, for he was my father. And on that day I was born, at that moment, there existed no love between Mr. Potter and Annie, for she was called only that then, Annie, though later she was called Miss Annie and then Annie Drew, but then she was called Annie, and Annie and Mr. Potter hated each other but it was a hatred with no real consequence for they had done nothing that would result in the death of each other, it was not a hatred with a power to harm either of them, it was only a hatred which caused me much suffering, a hatred which caused Mr. Potter to deny me the protection of his patrimony; a hatred which because I do not know their past as they had lived it together, their past when they had lived it apart from each other, their past when I was just a figure in the distance, a figure unknown to them; this hatred that existed between them became a part of my own life as I live it even today and I do not understand how this could be so, but it is true all the same. And Mr. Potter had no patrimony for he did not own himself, he had no private thoughts, he had no thoughts of wonder, he did not have a mind's eye in which he could wander, he had no thoughts about his past, his future, and his present which lay in between them both—his past and his future—and he was not ignorant, he was not without a conscience, he could not read and he could not write and he could not render the story of life, his own in particular, with coherency and I can read and I can write and I am his daughter.

And my own mother Annie Victoria Richardson left her home in Mahaut, Dominica, and she passed through the Windward Passage, which was a corridor of violent winds trapped in a swirling torrent of motion, moving, moving toward a cluster of islands, Antigua, Barbuda, St. Kitts, Nevis, and Anguilla, and she left Dominica on a boat with improperly mended sails and landed on the island of Antigua, the island where her own father, Alfred John Richardson, was born, and she left her home after a quarrel with her father over the way she should pursue her unfolding future, and after that quarrel, he made her dead in the realm of his fatherly love, he disinherited her. And why is it that joy, encountered unexpectedly and fully, will have at its core a replication of your own sorrow, will in the very near distance cause you to feel disemboweled, lost, as if your own self was somewhere else, while at the same time you can see yourself in front of you, you are far away and you are right there nearby and how lost, how lost you are and you go searching for that joy, that original joy, but your joy is your sorrow, your joy has not turned to sorrow, your joy was always sorrow, a form of sorrow, just sorrow.

And my mother Annie Victoria Richardson, her hair then, as a young woman of sixteen and then seventeen and then eighteen and then still a young woman at twenty-five when she met Mr. Potter, her hair then was long and black and waved down her back past her shoulders, and sometimes she wore her hair in two plaits pinned up around the crown of her head and sometimes she wore her hair captured in a black hairnet and the hairnet and the hair were the identical shade of black and her hair then seemed as if she had pinned the fat black tail of an unheard-of mammal at the nape of her neck. How beautiful she was then, I have been told so by her and by other people who knew her then, but not by Mr. Potter, for he never spoke to me of her, he never spoke to me of anything, he never spoke to me at all. And then when she was sixteen, and then seventeen, and then eighteen and up to just before she met Mr. Potter when she was twenty-five, she began living in the city of St.

John's in that place called Grays Farm and she lived in a house, a room really, with four windows and two doors and she lived all alone then, not with one child, girl or boy. She lived in this house all alone and got up every day for five days of the week and went off to work, sometimes keeping orderly the houses, proper houses, of people who needed and could afford such a thing, sometimes washing their clothes, sometimes bathing and feeding their children, but when she had been a girl and living under the harsh care of her father, he had sent her to school, he had insisted that she go to school, that she know how to read and write, and so eventually she grew tired of the houses that needed to be kept orderly and the people who lived in them and of the clothes they wore and their children and whether their children were hungry or dirty. She went to work in the surgery of a friend of her father's, a doctor, and then this doctor decided to go and live in St. Kitts, for all his wife's family were there, and my mother then went to work for Dr. Weizenger, scrubbing and sterilizing with boiling water the steel instruments he used for extracting teeth, scrubbing and sterilizing the needles and syringes he used for administering medicines of one kind or the other, making sure that the fingernails of the patients he would see were not dirty and that their hair was freshly combed and that they had just taken a bath and had just brushed their teeth, for all these things, if they were not just so, would make the doctor, Weizenger, irritable and sometimes they might make him so irritable that he would send the patient away, send the patient away without seeing him or her at all. And Dr. Weizenger practiced medicine, applying the little knowledge he had about the diseases of the mouth to dentistry, applying the little knowledge he had regarding childhood diseases to the illnesses that plagued children, applying the little knowledge he had of the workings of the mature human body to adult men and women who came to him with pain in their backs and heads and feet and all the other places where pain could be lodged in the human body; and he spoke English perfectly, but as if this language was lodged in the deepest recesses of his brain and was in some way hard to get to; he spoke English as if he was in pain, as if it was something he was being forced to do, and this was so, for Dr. Weizenger came from far away, from a place where the English language existed in another sphere, and in that place where he was from, he had taken up speaking English as a hobby, something to do in his spare time, something full of pleasure in the middle of the sad landscape into which he was born. And my mother Annie, who was not my mother yet and had not met Mr. Potter yet, but was my mother all the same, I can see that now, regarded Dr. Weizenger with much disdain, for he was ignorant and could not speak properly the language in which he found himself alive; she spoke English and French and a language that combined the two and she felt herself free and without boundaries and without obligations, but she was not without boundaries or obligations, she already was my mother and Mr. Potter was my father.

And my mother then was flames in her own fire, not waves in her own sea, she would be that later, after I was born and had become a grown woman, she would become that to me, an ocean with its unpredictable waves and undertow; she was then flames in her own fire and she was very beautiful and her beauty was mentioned sometimes with admiration and affection by others, sometimes with disapproval and scorn by some others, and it was as if her beauty was a blessing in the world sometimes, and as if her beauty was a sign of evil in the world sometimes. And when she was young my mother thought herself beautiful and loved being so and would invite other people into the atmosphere of her beauty and would, with her beauty, create little events that would make people who had witnessed her pause (she walked down the length of Scot's Row with her hair carelessly piled up on her head as if she had just stepped out of the darkness of her house without meaning for anyone to see her), and these people liked her and these people did not like her and there were many of them, one hundred or so. And in the middle of this, something that might become me appeared in her womb, clotting and swelling up, tissue which remained only tissue, for she would not allow it to become otherwise, she would not allow it to become me or anyone else, it would remain mere tissue in her womb. Four times this thickening of fluids gathered in her womb, four times before she was thirty years of age she managed to throw it out, and these fluids gathered up in her womb, clotting and then swelling and then were expelled before they became someone or something. And when my mother tried to force her menstruation unnaturally for the fifth time, she failed and that failure was because of me, I could not be expelled from my mother's womb at her own will. All this my mother told me when I was forty-one years of age and had by then become the mother of two children, the only two children my womb now will ever bear. And my mother was Annie Victoria Richardson, not my mother at all, not my mother yet, and she was my mother even so, for I was suspended within her, even though the world, which included her and Mr. Potter, did not know of me and did not know of the other thickenings and would never care for the thickened substance in her womb and eventually would never really care for me. But here I am and I can read and I can write my own name and much more than that, I now can tell myself of Mr. Potter in the written word and I now can tell Mr. Potter of his life with my mother Annie Victoria Richardson and Mr. Potter is now dead and so too is Annie, who came from Dominica to Antigua when she was sixteen years of age, against her father's wishes.

Temper it, temper it, I now say to myself as I sit here in the middle of the night, the dark blue and black of the night, blackest black of the night, the night so still, as if it had never known disruption, as if the most hideous and disturbing deeds had never occurred in the deep stillness of night: birth and death, being born and becoming dead, in the deep stillness that is the night, the blackest of black that is the night. And in my mind, I turn over Mr. Potter and Annie Victoria Richardson, and they are in my memory, though that does seem an impossibility, that I could have known them before I was born of the two of them, and yet it is so: I have in my mind a memory of them from before the time they became my mother and my father, and I can see them breathing at the time they were being born and struggling into living and being, and I can see them passing through their lives as children and then into being the two people who came together and made me, and through all of this I see them in substantial particularity and I see them as specters, possibilities of the real, possibilities of the real as it pertains to me. And my name when I was born then was Elaine Cynthia, and Annie Richardson was my mother, and that is my substantial particularity and Mr. Potter is my specter. Looking, looking, searching, searching, and I find that I am extraordinary and then I am not so at all, I find that I am the opposite of extraordinary, and then I find that I am spectacular and then I am not so at all, spectacular, that is; and the wind blows, and the sun shines, and the surface of the earth rises up and falls down in violent activity, and the inhabitants of the surface of the earth are often defeated by the shifting of the earth's varying and constantly changing contours, and my mother Annie Victoria Richardson and my father Roderick Potter were, just then, at the time before I would be born, and even at the time I was born, were without interest in the world, were without interest in the world and the forces that cause it to spin from one end to the other. And I, halfway to being myself, lay between my mother Annie Victoria Richardson and Roderick Nathaniel Potter, who really was my father. And the weight that I was then, and the volume of sound that I could make then, and the amount of space that I occupied then, and the extent to which I was conscious then, and the sorrow I knew then, and the absence of permanent joy or spontaneous joy or frequent joy—all of this has remained unchanged from then to now, as I write this; the contents and the volume and the weight of my joy and sorrow were the same then as they are now. And I believe now that all aspiration is futile and I knew then that to violently demand and make a change was essential and I see now that all change is its same self and all different selves are the same, and my father, Mr. Potter, could not read or write, and my mother, Annie Victoria Richardson, could read and write but did not think that the one had anything to do with the other, and so I can say to myself and I can say to anyone that this is that and that is a series of things, all of them wrong and all of them never to be resolved satisfactorily, and all wrongs inspire justice and then again all wrongs will eventually succumb to defeat. "You can com' go Mooma, you can com' go Poopa," Mr. Potter sang to himself as he drove Mr. Shoul's car, as he walked to his job as a driver of a taxi that belonged to Mr. Shoul, as he walked from the house which was only one room with four windows and two doors and in this house lived one woman or another and they had borne him girl children. Or Mr. Potter sang, "Pennywheeler! Uhm, hmmmm, hmmmm, hmmmm, hmmmm, hmmmm, hmmmm Pennywheeler! Uhm, hmmmm, hmmmm, hmmmm, hmmmm, hmmmm, hmmmm Pennywheeler," repeating the words to this tune over and over, as he tossed a farthing into the air and always caught it with the king's profile facing up, or as he stood before a looking glass and with his hand tried to make his rigidly curled hair stay close to his scalp, or as he buckled his belt, or as he listened to the end-less stream of memories that Mr. Shoul had of the

Lebanon and going back and forth to Syria and parts of the world nearby. And "Why ya, why ya, why ya lef you big fat pomm-pomm outside, lef you pomm-pomm outside, lef you pomm-pomm outside, why ya lef you big fat pomm-pomm outside," sang Mr. Potter, to himself and only to himself, as he went to see a woman who had not yet become the mother of one of his many girl children, or as he went to see the mother of one of his girl children but the child was somewhere else, as if she had not yet been born and if she was born, as if it had never been so. And all the songs that he sang to himself, and all the songs as they went through his head in silence, meant nothing, they were only something random that occupied his mind and then again all of them meant something, but what? Mr. Potter did not care to know an answer.

And on all the days of Mr. Potter's life the sun shone, even when it rained the sun shone, for the sun was a constant, if it went away for three hundred and sixty-five days, it would remain constant, for it was all that made up this landscape. And it was all Mr. Potter would ever know ever, it was all Mr. Potter would ever know, and the sun, a planetary body, indifferent to the significance or insignificance of individuals and Mr. Potter's ups and downs, shone down in its usual way, with a heat so ferocious that it could bear up or tear down a person, and Mr. Potter walked through his days that were sunlight and his nights that were dark with waiting for the sun, and the gentleness that is sometimes part of life would embrace Mr. Potter but he did not know that; and the harsh brutality that was life reigned over Mr. Potter, reigned not like an earthly monarch who would come and go, but like something celestial.

And Mr. Potter experienced the depths of feeling that made up life and the smooth surfaces of pleasant exchanges that made up life in the same way, "Eh, eh, me ah tell you mahn," and he straightened his cap and ran one of his fingers across the collar of his shirt and smoothed down the front of his pants and took some saliva from his mouth and smeared it across his shoes and his cheeks and the world was so nice and how everything all went his way, for he, even he, had a way and my mother interrupted it. This way, this world, of Mr. Potter's, with its smooth turns and steady revolving of the mothers of his girl children and their lives, mothers and girl children, all swathed up in a cocoon that would never burst open and metamorphose into anything other than what it already was, all this way of certainties is what my mother interrupted. And my mother, herself already a series of beautifully poisonous eruptions, a boiling cauldron of strange fluids, a whirlwind of sex and passion and female beauty and deception and pain and female humiliation and narcissism and vulnerability, met Mr. Potter as he stood in the vicinity of Mr. Shoul and Mr. Shoul's cars and the street, which was named after a king of England or a saint from somewhere, George or Mary, and I, writing all this now, came into being just at that moment and I, who am writing all this now, came into being a very long time before that.

And that morning, when the sun was in its usual place, somewhere between the east and west horizons, Drickie and Annie, my father and my mother, met, and they lived together at Points, in a house that was only one room, quarreled, and when my mother was seven months pregnant with me, she took all of Mr. Potter's savings, money he had stored in a crocus bag under their bed, money he had been saving to one day buy his own car and become the driver of his own taxi, and she left with me growing at the normal rate of a baby in her stomach, and went to live all by herself in another house that was really one room and this house was in Grays Farm. And those last harsh words my mother and father, Annie and Drickie, said to each other, and her murderous action directed at him, taking the money he had saved, with which he meant to make of himself some semblance of a man, and her leaving him to perish again and again each new day in the world of Mr. Shoul, led to Mr. Potter's never seeing my face when I was newly born or anytime soon after, and led to my having a line drawn through me, that space where Mr. Potter's name ought to be is not full with my father and his name, it is not empty either, it only has a line drawn through it, and that line is drawn through me. And this inheritance I have passed on to no one, I have never claimed it, I have never done anything with it except to look and turn it over in my mind and make note of it, I have passed it on to no one. My name, Elaine Cynthia Potter, crossed out by the line that was drawn through it, I first abandoned and then changed to something else altogether, so that the line drawn through me, now, cannot find me, and if it did, would not recognize me, and that line cannot see me, but I can see it, following me each day as I do some ordinary thing, breathing in and out, for instance, or gazing out a window watching a soft rain fall, for instance, or removing from the palm of my hand the almost fatal lance of an unusual insect, for instance. The line that is drawn through me, this line I have inherited, but I have not accepted my inheritance and so have not deeded it to anyone who shall follow me.

And when I was born, in the very early morning of a Wednesday, five o'clock, the sun was not in the middle of the sky then, it was only just below the horizon, only just beginning its ordinary journey to the middle of the sky, to the middle of the day, so tiresome to an observer, so indifferent to being observed, and when I was born, newly out of my mother's womb, I did not cry, and that was to be the signal that I was alive, but I did not cry and the woman assisting my mother in my being born slapped me, lightly to her and suiting her cruel understanding of the world, but hard to me, just newly born and with no experience or understanding of the world into which I had just entered, and I cried and cried, loud, louder, and more loudly than ever and that strong cry was later described to me as evidence of a strong character, likable when I was just born, but not at all so now. And my mother's name then was Annie Victoria Richardson and my father's name then was Roderick Potter, but only Annie claimed me and this woman, Annie Richardson, held me close to her breast and fed me milk and that was all she had to offer me then, the thin, clear, milky fluid that was called milk, flowing out from the enlarged pores of her breast. And she fed me and fed me her milk and I drank it and drank it and then one day her breasts ran dry, no milk came out of them, and this is just what she said to me when I was three years old and five years old and then seven years old, and then after a time she no longer told me that story, of how she fed me her milk until I sucked her dry, and I reminded her of this one day when I myself had children and had grown tired of feeding them milk from my breast, and my mother said that she did not remember telling me that I had drained her of milk and in any case, she said, such a thing never happened and could not have happened since she could not remember it happening so. And I can see myself in a photograph when I was seven years old, and from seeing my face, I look vacant, from looking at my face, I seem as if I am without content of any kind, but it is only the absence of Mr. Potter that is written on my face; I have a line drawn through me, and that overwhelms everything that I know about myself at this moment, that line overwhelms the milk I drank from my mother's breast and my mother's name was Annie Victoria Richardson and it was she and my father Roderick Potter who made me.

And I can see my face, it is in my mind's eye, and my cheeks are round and fat like Elfrida Robinson's and my nose is fat and thick and spreads out toward and then rests on my cheeks and the plumpness of my cheeks is exactly like that of Elfrida Robinson's and the exact plumpness of my nose occurs in identical form on the face of Nathaniel Potter and this nose also appears on the face of Mr. Potter and all the girl children he fathered. All the girl children Mr. Potter fathered had such a nose, a nose that resembled his own and through his nose he knew with certainly that he was their father. And Mr. Potter said "Eh, eh, eh, eh" when seeing these girls, and sometimes he said it with pleasure, because they had recently been born and he still favored their mothers, and sometimes he said it with annoyance, for he could remember their mothers' annoying ways with their demands on him, and always he said it in anger when those girls who were born and would die with the shape of Mr. Potter's nose dominating the smooth contour that was their face appeared standing in front of him and asked him for something essential, something essential other than the part he had played in their very coming into existence. Schoolbooks, for instance, not underthings or a hat, but schoolbooks. One day when I was about four years old, the age at which reality and apprehension of reality and bewilderment and uncertainty made up my world completely, I stood in the shadow of Mr. Shoul's garage and waited for Mr. Potter, who was at that time busily ferrying passengers from one place to another in Mr. Shoul's taxi, and one of those passengers was Dr. Weizenger all by himself then, he was not with his wife, and I waited and waited, and waiting seemed so natural to me then, as if it were the sky or the land or oxygen or rainwater, so seemed waiting to me; and I waited for Mr. Potter, and his friend George Martin said he would not come, but I waited all the same, and then Mr. Potter came, driving a car with the brand Hillman or Zephyr stamped on it, and when he saw me, he waved me away as if I were an abandoned dog blocking his path, as if I were nothing to him at all and had suddenly and insanely decided to pursue an intimate relationship with him. "Eh, eh," said Mr. Potter. And my life began, absent Mr. Potter, in the dimly lit ward of the Holberton Hospital, with my mother's resentment silently beaming at him, with my mother's love for me and my mother's resentment silently beaming at me, and then I was swathed in yards of white cotton and laid to rest in the pose of the newborn which is also the pose of the dead, my eyes closed, my arms folded firmly across my chest, my entire body stilled, but I was not dead, my chest moved up and down, ever so slightly for I was just newly born and my lungs were getting used to the process of first going in and then going out. And I lay beside my mother in the Holberton Hospital, nestled close to her breast, drinking my first nourishment, her milk, and she lay next to me, feeding me my first nourishment, the milk that had been stored in her breast, and how she loved me as she fed me, and how she hated the person who was part of the process of her feeding me, Mr. Potter, and he was my father. And from the Holberton Hospital, my mother, Annie Victoria Richardson, took me, whom by that time she had named Elaine, after a daughter of Mr. Shoul's, and that name, Elaine, had no meaning to Mr. Shoul at all, but to my mother it was a name she had heard Mr. Shoul's daughter being called, and my mother had loved Mr. Shoul's chauffeur, that would have been Mr. Potter, and my mother now loved me, but after I was born she never saw Mr. Potter or Mr. Shoul or Mr. Shoul's daughter, except in passing, and so for a long time in my life I bore the name of people my mother no longer liked or loved or even wished well and from the Holberton Hospital she took me to Grays Farm, into a house which was really only one room with some windows and two doors. And as I grew from only a newborn, going into the first full year of my life, the milk from my mother's breast was augmented with porridge made of cornmeal or arrowroot. And I grew all the same, and could talk before I could walk and I was a marvel to see, a marvel to observe, but Mr. Potter never saw me then, not when I was a baby and in need of him, not when I was a little girl and in need of him, Mr. Potter never saw me at all, for he had caused a line to be drawn through me, and my mother, using her formidable will, anger, and imagination, had driven a sharp knife into the heart of Mr. Potter and that heart was the little bundle of money meant to be the beginning of a life Mr. Potter had in mind for himself, and in that way another line was born, this line was drawn between me and Mr. Potter and that line was firm and for our whole lives it remained unbreachable and love could not touch it, for hatred and indifference were its name.

And I come back to Mr. Potter again and again, he with his chauffeur's cap worn jauntily on his head, his shirt well ironed, the crease down the front of his trousers stiffly in place, his teeth gleaming in the harsh light of the sun, for he had scrubbed them with the tip of a damp cloth dipped in ashes, his black chauffeur's shoes gleaming from the rough rubbing he had administered to them, his words emerging from his mouth consoling and soothing Mr. Shoul, who every day was entangled in some memory of olive groves and the road to Damascus and hurriedly leaving the Lebanon and trying to settle in Surinam and trying to settle in Trinidad and suitcases filled with pots and pans and yard upon yard of different kinds of coarse cloth and lace; and Mr. Potter's words emerging from his mouth were consoling and soothing to the many passengers he ferried from one part of the island of Antigua to another, and these passengers denounced climates not known to Mr. Potter, climates in which they lived and so therefore hated, and they asked him about the things to be seen through the windows of the taxi: the fields of sugarcane, and just a quick glance revealed the hardship of labor involved in cultivating it, the fields of cotton plants in flower, and just a quick glance revealed the hardship of labor involved in cultivating and bringing it to harvest, the mud houses with straw roofs, the torn clothes drying on the clotheslines, the half-naked children with swollen stomachs, the indescribable and invisible lushness that they could feel enveloping them; and Mr. Potter would say, "Yes, Yes, Yes!" and the "Yes" would be so drawn out, would take so long to come to an end, that perhaps a journey could be made around the world in its entirety before these many "Yeses" were completed. And Mr. Potter's voice was so consoling and soothing, as if he were an undertaker, embalming each memory of Mr. Shoul's, each observation of his passengers', and doing so without really taking them in, they were all nothing to him, they were only part of what life had visited upon him, and Mr. Shoul would one day go, and Dr. Weizenger would one day go and the passengers in the taxi would one day go, and Mr. Potter would remain forever after they had gone, for he had given meaning to this landscape, the sea, the sun shining so brightly in the middle of the noonday sky, the huge black-colored wind, blowing from the windward direction, devouring the sun that had been so perfectly placed within the noonday sky. He had given meaning to the abolition of forced servitude, he had given meaning to picnics on Whitsunday, something that was revolting to Dr. Weizenger—Whitsunday—but a holiday that gave Mr. Shoul an excuse to eat more than usual.

For this world of Mr. Potter's, with its desires fulfilled and its desires thwarted (and, unknown to Mr. Potter, it was a familiar pattern to most human beings), this world of his was a constantly boiling cauldron of bad and good, but the good things boiled more rapidly and disappeared quickly, evaporating and going up in wisps and then vanishing altogether in the air, and the bad things boiled and boiled, sending up froth and bubbles, and the bad things boiled and boiled, forever and ever and increased in volume. And

Mr. Potter's self, after a day of being in his car, filled up with false goodwill toward people he would never really know and people he did not wish to really know, and the earth itself revolved as usual on its axis and it was beyond indifference to Mr. Potter's existence; and it was the end of his day with Mr. Shoul, Dr. Weizenger, and the people who came from climates they did not like and who had made for themselves a regular escape from this climate they did not like altogether, and Mr. Potter exhaled loudly a soft sound, a sigh, and he went from the day's end at Mr. Shoul's garage to the many houses which were really one room with four windows and he could see all the women who were the mothers of his girl children and all of those girls with his broad and fleshy nose, and he looked at his children, all of them girls, and he looked at their mothers, women who longed for his presence and for his presence to remain a constant day after day, and that when he went away he would return with the same intensity and self-possession as when he left. And they longed for his presence, and they longed for his presence over and over, and how they wanted his presence to be permanent. But Mr. Potter's caresses and embraces were like a razor and each woman and girl child of his who had received one of his embraces was left with skin shredded and hanging toward the floor and blood falling down to meet the floor and bones exposed and sinew, too, and nerves;

and after all that, the person, the mother with her girl child, was recomposed, not made new, only recomposed into an ordinary mother with her girl child, and their tears could make a river and their sighs of sorrow and regret could make mountains, and the pangs of hunger in their stomachs could make a verdant valley, and they cried to Mr. Potter, these children and their mothers who lived in houses which were really a single room with four windows, and their tears fell like fat sheets of rain and their cries made no difference, no difference at all to anybody.

And here are the many interstices of Mr. Potter's heart: valleys of regret and hope and disappointment; mountains of regret and hope and disappointment; seas of longing; plains barren of vegetation and plains full of dust; shallow gutters of joy; deep crevices of sorrow; a sharp ledge of awe. So went the interstices of Mr. Potter's heart and all of this was a secret to him and so sometimes he sang with joy a song about a man running after a woman as she skipped through brambles and sugarcane fields unscathed and this woman would taunt her pursuer with sounds she created in the largest part of her throat, and Mr. Potter only sang a song about this, such a thing had never happened to him. And sometimes again he sang a hymn about the ending of the day, the ending of life itself, and the many secrets of God hidden in everything large and small, but he only sang the hymn with a determination he did not allow himself to know, he kept the meaning of the hymn hidden from himself. And the interstices of Mr. Potter's heart resembled the surface of some familiar but not yet found planet, something so ordinary, something so rare.

And I am now the central figure in Mr. Potter's life as he has been in mine without either of us knowing it. I have known from even a time before I knew my own self that the central figure in my life was my mother Annie Victoria Richardson, but she is not a central figure in Mr. Potter's life, in Mr. Potter's life she is only one of the many women who lived in a house that was really a room with four windows and two doors and was the mother of one of his many girl children, and she was my mother and my name was Elaine Cynthia Potter, a name she gave to me. From dry land, see the lights of a ship as it makes its way through the black waters that are the sea; from the ever fretful surface of the earth, look up and see the benign brightness that makes up the stars; from across Redcliff Street, I, then a child with my name Elaine Cynthia Potter, saw Mr. Potter, Roderick was his name, Drickie was the name people who loved him and knew him very well called him, and this man, Mr. Potter, Roderick, and Drickie, was my father. And that name, Potter, haunted me when I was a child, for I did not know any Potters, I knew of a village called Potters but I had never met anyone who came from that place, and that name, Potter, was a part of my own name and yet I had never met the man whose name I bore. I saw him from across the street and from across the street I asked him for money to buy books that I needed for school, but I do not remember any of this, it is only that my mother has told me so and my mother's tongue and the words that flow from it cannot be relied upon, she is now dead. And who was I then, Potter or Richardson, for though my mother wove herself around me, wound me up in a cocoon of love and bitterness and anger and pain, and from this cocoon I shall never emerge, having metamorphosed into something new, something not yet heard of, something that might inspire desire and envy, entrapment and then death, through those unbreakable fibers I could feel Mr. Potter, the shadow of him, the real body of him, for he was my father and so he was in me, he was one of the elements in the emotional fibers that my mother had woven around me, but his presence was a shadow and that shadow had more substance than any real person I actually knew, and a real person was made up of blood and tissue and veins and arteries and organs and soft matter, but in my life Mr. Potter was a shadow, a shadow more important than any person I might know, a shadow more important than any apparition I would ever come to know. And then I became myself and Mr. Potter remained himself and the women who were the mothers of his many girl children remained the same, hating him and speaking ill of him, and my own mother spoke ill of him, this man whom she called Potter sometimes and Drickie less often, and when I was in her presence, the ill way in which she spoke of him was not addressed to me, it was addressed to an invisible audience, and I grew used to hearing my mother speak ill of a man named Potter and Drickie, a man I did not know and had never met, and yet I had met him and did know him, for an entire half of me was made wholly of him.

And Mr. Potter continued to wend his way into the world, how he continued to wend his way into the world, his world, his immediate and real world, not his world as a metaphor, and this world into which he continued to wend his way was shaped by men and other people and events, some deliberate and some accidental; for Mr. Shoul's displacement was deliberate but his presence in Mr. Potter's life was an accident, and the attempt to murder Dr. Weizenger was planned but Mr. Potter becoming his chauffeur was an accident. And while living within the maze of the accidental and the deliberate, Mr. Potter met and married a woman named Yvonne. And Yvonne had a child, a girl, and they, Yvonne and her girl child, lived with Mr. Potter in a house with many rooms and each room had more than one window and each window was made up of four pieces of glass pane and each window was framed with curtains and the curtains were made of cotton on which had been printed the images of hibiscus in bloom and birds, just birds, in flight, all in colors and sizes that were not known in the natural world. And then Yvonne had another child, a boy this time, but Mr. Potter was not his father, Mr. Potter was not the father of this little boy, the father of this little boy was a fashionable undertaker in the city of St. John's, Antigua, and Mr. Potter loved his son, and the father of his son was someone who administered to the dead and Mr. Potter loved his son best of all his children and all his real children were girls and he was the father of all these many girls but he did not love them, he only loved his son whose real father was a fashionable and well-regarded undertaker. And Yvonne would place her children in a perambulator and parade them around the shady parts of town, taking a stroll with them along East Street when the flamboyant trees were full of flowers so full, as if flowers were all they would bear, and she would wheel her children around the botanical garden, stopping to rest (but she did not need a rest at all) at the rubber tree, a specimen of vegetable matter so far away from the place in which it had originated, as were the perambulator and the curtains and the panes of glass that made up her windows, and Mr. Shoul and Dr. Weizenger.

Oh, to see a life, so small, so vulnerable at its beginning, so soft and sweet to touch and taste at its beginning, so wingless yet in flight, so much a part of this world yet so unbeholden to it at its beginning. Oh, to see a human being new, freshly made, with all of life ahead, a stout bolt of carefully woven linen, with weft crossing warp in perfection, and this bolt of carefully woven linen is unsmudged and undirtied in any way, and as it unrolls, as it unfolds, yard after yard, it is filled with images that make up love and joy and contentment and all this to such a degree that even sorrow and disappointment and pain are only a form of this love and joy and contentment and how manageable and to be agreed on as the world in all its entirety would be if it was made up in just this way, a large bolt of clean cloth, unrolling and unrolling and each unrolling becoming filled up with images of love and so on and so on, until the bolt was finished, not cut into after many yards but just finished, and there was nothing left on the staff that had made up the foundation of a life, the life to be seen at its beginning. And there was Mr. Potter, my father, a certainty even then, lying deep within his own father Nathaniel and lying deep within his own mother, Elfrida Robinson, and I lying even deeper inside them. And from Nathaniel and Elfrida came Mr. Potter and then me, and the bolt of cloth continues to unfold and no one has made a cut in it and it has not yet come to an end, for even though Mr. Potter slammed the door in my face when I was sent by my mother to ask him for a tablet of writing paper, I still managed to acquire the ability to read and the ability to write and in this way I make Mr. Potter and in this way I unmake Mr. Potter, and apart from the fact that he is now dead, he is unable to affect the portrait of him I am rendering here, the scenes on the bolt of cloth as he appears in them: the central figure.

And so in the middle of his life, for he was born in nineteen hundred and twenty-two and he died in nineteen hundred and ninety-two, Mr. Potter was the father of many girl children and the father of only one boy and that boy was not his, in truth, in actual fact, that boy's father was the second most important undertaker on the island of Antigua, and that little boy, whose name was Louis, and he was named after someone who had been a king, was fat and indolent and unpleasant; his real father was just the opposite of Mr. Potter, for Mr. Potter was not acquainted with the meal of worms or other parasites who lived beneath the earth. And Mr. Potter loved that little boy who was not his own and was not like him in any way, for this little boy was a boy so empty he was even empty of emptiness itself, and at the school he attended he kicked a ball and the ball missed its goal, and at the school he attended he was always last or near last in scholarly ranking and in a footrace he always lagged far behind everyone and he had an abundance of schoolbooks and tablets of writing paper packed securely in a traditional schoolbag, and he had more than enough food to eat at home and his clothes always smelled freshly washed and his hair was cleaned and combed daily, and all that made up this boy's young life was wonderful and seemingly complete, so wonderful and seemingly complete that anyone observing it, and I am thinking of a particular anyone, me as a child, me as myself now looking at myself as a child, would only, could only, feel longing; longing for such a wonderful life, longing for such completeness, longing to completely belong and in such a wonderful way. Mr. Potter so loved his son and his son was named Louis and his son was not really of him, he was only a boy whose mother was Mr. Potter's wife, Yvonne was her real name, and Louis was born early in the night and the moon was full and that moon was so full of light and the light spilled out onto the sky and colored the clouds in such a way that they seemed like habitable islands, and that moon so overly filled with light made mysterious and magical all the landscapes over which it traveled, and that moon was full and full of light and then that moon grew smaller and smaller and its light grew weaker and weaker and so did Louis, as if the moon, which by happenstance was the moon in the sky on the night he was born, was his destiny. And Louis lived to be forty-five years old and did nothing that mattered, really, and then he died of a lung ailment or of a disease of the intestinal tract, I do not know which exactly, and the moon under which he was born retreated and for Louis it remained so, never rising again and never waning again, and then, at forty-five years old, Louis died in Canada. And by the time Louis died, Mr. Potter had died also, and at the time Mr. Potter died he had no idea that Louis's death would so soon follow his own, and at the time of Mr. Potter's death Louis did not know that so soon after he too would be dead. And as I write of their living and dying and as I read what I have written about their living and dying, I do not know the end of my living and the beginning of my dying, for they—living and dying—are both mixed up.

And Mr. Potter did not have a uterus that shuddered in agony, for he was a man, and he did not have a menstrual cycle, for he was man, and he did not have ovaries that when discharging an egg which had not been fertilized caused him to feel pain in the area below his waist and above his pelvis, for Mr. Potter was a man and not a woman. Mr. Potter was a man and he was my father and I never knew him at all, had never touched him, or known how he smelled after a night of sleep or after a full day's work, or the smell of his breath after eating a special kind of food, or the look of him after he had an ordinary experience that related to touching or smelling or seeing or hearing. I have only a vague memory of him ignoring me as I passed him by in the street, of him slamming a door in my face when I was sent to ask him for money I needed to purchase my writing paper, and the full knowledge of the line drawn through me which I inherited from him, and this line drawn through me binds me to him even as it was very much meant to show that I did not belong to him, that I belonged to no one male, that I did not have a father, that no one had fathered me, and that I was female and came from the female line and belonged to my mother and to my mother only.

And Mr. Potter did not move toward his end swiftly and inexorably, oh no, not at all, not in that way at all. Mr. Potter moved toward his end in an unhurried way, driving one of the three cars he eventually came to own through the streets of the city of St. John's, leaving the streets of the city of St. John's and driving a passenger who had just disembarked from an airplane or a large ship out toward the village of Emanuel and then going through Jennings and Liberta and Falmouth and Swetes and Freetown and Newfield and Bethesda and Old Road and Urlings and John Hughes and Parham and up to Barnes Hill and Cedar Grove and Table Hill Gordon and then home to All Saints Road where he lived in a house with his wife Yvonne and Louis, who was not really his son, and another child who did not count at all for she was a girl child and he had so many of those. For after my mother had left him, taking with her me, seven months in her stomach, and all of Mr. Potter's savings which he had kept in a crocus bag tucked under the mattress of their bed, he had started all over again at Mr. Shoul's garage, and after that incident, after my mother left him and stole all that was valuable to him, his money, especially his money, which was his future, he went to his work at Mr. Shoul's as if it was his first day, as if he had never done it before, as if it was new to him, and he worked and worked and saved his money and then bought a car of his own and with the profits from that bought another car and hired a driver and with the profits from that bought another car and hired another driver, and not once did he imagine that he was imitating Mr. Shoul, not once did Mr. Shoul's life enter his imagination, for Mr. Potter did in a vague way know that Mr. Shoul did not make the world turn, the world had turned and Mr. Shoul became dislodged from his place in it, the road to Damascus, and the Lebanon and Palestine and date trees and olive groves and so much strangeness, so Mr. Potter thought, so much strangeness.

And Mr. Potter did not move toward his death swiftly and inexorably, and he did not leave Mr. Shoul's employ in that way either. It was in Mr. Shoul's household that he met my mother, Annie Victoria Richardson, where she worked as the nursemaid taking care of Mr. Shoul's children; one of them, a girl, was named Elaine, and my mother, to demon-strate to this small girl her power to transform the world, said that she would bear a child, a girl, and name that girl Elaine. And without knowing any of this, I hated my name and planned to change it every day of my life until the day I did do so. And I now do not hate the name Elaine, I only now, even now, still hate the person who named me so, and that person is now dead. My mother is dead. And she moved toward her own death swiftly and inexorably even though she was alive eighty years.

And I am wondering now if there was a romance of some sort between them and I can imagine that the answer is yes, because I can see my mother's own beautiful long black shiny hair, which she wore all rolled and pinned up on top of her head so that it lay there like a loaf of bread, and I imagine my father, that is, Mr. Potter, seeing his face reflected in that tightly wound braid of hair, and loving his reflection and loving the object that caused his reflection to gaze back at him. And I wonder if there was love between them and the answer to that would be no, because my mother would not submit to anything, certainly not to love, with all its chaos, its demands, its unpredictabil-ity; and because Mr. Potter could not love anyone, not anyone who was his own. And he loved the boy Louis, but Louis was not his own son.

Oh, how slowly night falls, how imperceptibly night begins, for night begins when the sun is in its usual place, up above and in the middle of the sky, and shining so harshly bright it makes shadows pale. Night begins in the middle of the day. And I was thirty-three years old and living in a city that was between thirty and forty-five degrees latitude north of the equator. And my life, as I viewed it then, was in a tunnel, ablaze with torrents of fire, and there were no exits; and at that time I glowed not like an ember surging toward ashes but like a stout log enveloped in flames. And Mr. Potter hovered over it, my life, with his line drawn through me and I was alive and would be for a long time, a time beyond his imagining. And at that time, when I was thirty-three years old and living north of the equator and in the temperate zone, he came into my life like a dying insect drawn to a heated glassy surface, or like a dying insect drawn to the stilled surface of a pool of water. He was dying then and I was living in a place far from where I was born, comfortably. But how was I to know that he was dying, for he did not tell me, he did not know it himself. And Mr. Potter and I were standing in a room with three windows and the room was in a house and the house had many rooms and each room had at least two windows, sometimes three windows, sometimes four windows, but each room was part of this entire house in which I now lived. And I was thirty-three years of age, my life then far removed from its origins in Mr. Potter and my mother Annie Victoria Richardson and Mr. Shoul and Dr. Weizenger, who had tended me when I came down with a case of typhoid fever and whooping cough even though he knew nothing about childhood ailments, he had been trained to be a psychiatrist, but in Antigua no one had ever heard of such a thing as a psychiatrist. And my life was far removed from Mr. Potter and my illegitimate claim to my patrimony through him. A light filled the room, it was not a natural light, it did not come from the sun in its usual place, up above and in the middle of the sky, and shining so harshly bright that it would make even the shadows tremble; this light that filled the room was made up of fear and mistrust and anger and disappointment and a small number of questions: why? For a small number would be better than a large number. But nothing goes along smoothly for too long, not even the unsmooth itself, and so the light that was made up of fear and other things that cause discomfort vanished, and Mr. Potter told me that from looking at me he realized that all his girl children had his nose, he said all my girl children have my nose, and I then suddenly saw a set of faces, not a sea, but a set, of faces, their eyes closed, their mouths clasped shut, their nostrils open, two small holes, as if offering a view into an eternity of some kind. And Mr. Potter said this: when looking at me, he realized that all his girl children had the same nose as his own, and my own nose, which had never seemed of any consequence to me at all, suddenly grew into a mountain as it rested on the base that was my face, and it overwhelmed every other aspect of the small area that was my face and my face no longer existed, just for that moment, that span of time that lasted while Mr. Potter told me that through my nose he recognized me as one of his children, a girl, and in truth he had only girl children.

And why not the eyes, I said to myself then and even now, why not the eyes, which are sometimes said to offer a way of entering the soul, and why not the ears, which are sometimes said to offer a way of entering into the eternally celestial, and why not the mouth, which is sometimes said to be the instrument through which the imagined, the world held in the mind's eye, is brought to life through words. But only through the instrument of smell could Mr. Potter recognize his children, and those children were all female and those children were not familiar to each other, only Mr. Potter could make their noses and only through him and with him could they make sense of the world in which they found themselves. And how glad I was to be alive and to hear Mr. Potter say that I was his and my nose was his and I was his through his nose, and how much more important that was than if he had seen me or heard me, or touched me in some way or tasted me, which could never even be done, to taste me, and he spun himself into a golden ecstasy on the realization and the revelation that all his female offspring could be identified through their noses being similar to his own. And the light grew dim and then darkened and then completely disappeared because in the middle of everything I found my voice, not my nose, which was there and dominated everything and would not go away, but my voice, and I said to Mr. Potter, who was standing across from me in only one of the many rooms in which I lived then: What should I call you? How should I address you? What is your name to me? When wanting your attention, how can I get it? And I asked him plainly in this straightforward way: What am I to call you?

And that very question itself, What am I to call you? seemed to rearrange not only a singular world but a whole system of planetary revolutions, for in that simple statement, and it was a statement, not a question, I raised the issue of what he was to all these girls and what he was to himself and who was he to me as he stood before me in that room, one of many in the house in a city in the temperate zone. And my nose was on my face and the words What am I to call you? were in my mouth and then on my lips and then in the air that hung between us and surrounded us and suddenly I was overcome by a fear of mammals with wings and that fear was not explainable for I was in a city and it was daytime, I was not in an unmapped forest at night. And at that moment, should anger have surged through me like a force unpredictable in nature, should I have wished my father dead, should I have gone beyond mere wishing and walked over to him and grabbed him by the throat and squeezed his neck until his body lay limp at my feet, should I have thrown him out the window and then looked to see him lying in a lifeless, decorative puddle of blood, tissue, and bones on the sidewalk, should I have wished him somewhere else and something else and not related to me in any way at all at that very moment?

And I did wish him dead and I did want him dead and I wanted my moments past, present, and future to be absent of him, but he did not die then and I never saw him again and again or ever again and then he died.

And he left my life then forever, his back disappearing through the door of the house in which I lived, his back disappearing up the street on which stood the house in which I lived; and his appearance was like his absence, leaving my surface untroubled, causing not so much as the tiniest ripple, leaving only an empty space inside that is small when I am not aware of its presence and large when I am.

And Mr. Potter returned to his life, the smooth, everydayness of it, the ordinariness of it, breathing in, then breathing out, pulling his shirt over his head so that he could wear it and then pulling his shirt over his head so that he could remove it after wearing it, and his favorite meals were placed before him and he ate them and he moved through the streets of St. John's in a car made somewhere in North America, a car to him still seemed so magical, appearing in all its completeness and ready-to-be-carness, without at all betraying how it came to be that, a car. And Mr. Potter's life had been like that to him. Sometimes, if he had thought about it, sometimes his life had been like his car, made somewhere else, appearing as if by magic out of nowhere and without at all betraying how it came to be; that is how his life appeared to him sometimes, but he could not read and he could not write and all of his life and all of his feelings were trapped in a capsule which from time to time he could see in a glimmer, fleetingly, with certainty and then the opposite of certainty. And he could not read and he could not write and his life lay still, for he could not make wars or cause events to make a violent reversal. He made female children and all of them had noses that resembled his own.

And all the silvery twilight in the world did not fall on the top of Mr. Potter's head, and all the silvery twilight in the world did not fall on his shoulders, and he receded back into the world from which I had come and the world I did not know and so can still even now only yearn for, and he receded into the world from which he had come and knew so well, into the world of driving automobiles whose backseats were larger than the beds in which his daughters were conceived, and these automobiles offered a form of comfort which was unknown to Mr. Potter, getting from one place to another while thinking of something else altogether, something not having to do with the journey at all. And Mr. Potter receded into his own world, which was his life, and he turned his back to the world, the world as it is made up of that great big thing: a shared commonality, feelings of love for something ordinary, like his own child regardless of the shape of her nose, and the sun which shone overhead day after day, and the earth beneath his feet which could be forced to yield sustenance, and in between was the atmosphere in which he actually lived. And Eh, eh is what Mr. Potter said to himself, and "Eh, eh" is what Mr. Potter said out loud sometimes.

And walking along Market Street one day, a holiday, a special day designated to commemorate an event full of significance in the history of Mr. Potter's long-standing and overwhelming subjugation, Mr. Potter looked up and saw Mr. Shoul looking down on him from the veranda of Mr. Shoul's house, and Mr. Shoul was accompanied by his wife, who also came from the Lebanon or Syria or someplace near there, and she too had come to this place, Antigua, through some disaster made not by nature or anyone she loved, and she and Mr. Shoul and their children, especially one named Elaine, looked down on Mr. Potter and Mr. Potter looked up at them and all those gazes met, not as if in some celestial alignment, but in its complete opposite, random and evil and without purpose. And Mr. Potter walked on and by his side was a woman and she was a nurse by profession and she could not bear children through her own will. And how he walked, and walked and walked, through his own life again and again; and looking upward again he saw Dr. Weizenger, and his wife, who was a nurse also but from England, was with him but they had no children of any kind, not boys or girls, because the two of them were not fertile, or had decided not to be fertile, I do not know. And in the middle of New-gate Street was where Market Street came to an end, and above this juncture stood the Anglican cathedral and it had been built by African slaves, from whom Mr. Potter could trace his ancestors, and the tower of the cathedral had a clock with four faces look-ing north, south, east, and west, making the cathedral seem as if it simultaneously captured and released time, but all this notion of time captured and released was of no interest to Mr. Potter if only because he was all by himself: a definition of time captured and released, released and captured. And Dr. Weizenger, Zoltan was his name and Samuel was his name also, was often in the shadow of that clock, sometimes all by himself, sometimes with his wife, and that clock with its four sides, each facing one of the four corners of the earth, was meant to replicate another marker of time, the clock called Big Ben, situated in the capital city of London, or so thought Dr. Weizenger, but not

Mr. Potter, and Mr. Shoul thought only of the road that went toward and away from Damascus.

And that great big clock with its four sides, each facing one of the four corners of the earth, struck every hour on the hour, marking off time, as it passed, and the ending of each hour was the beginning of the next, and the clock had done that from the day of its completion by the hands of slaves, Mr. Potter's ancestors, hundreds of years before. And time was Dr. Weizenger's enemy: the past certainly; the future he did not know how that would turn out. And Mr. Potter's lifetime began in the year fourteen hundred and ninety-two but he was born on the seventh day of January, nineteen hundred and twenty-two, and his mother was Elfrida Robinson of English Harbour and his father was Nathaniel Potter, also of English Harbour, and the midwife who assisted his mother in bringing him into the world was named Nurse Eudelle. And all through this small narrative of this small life was the loud and harsh ringing of the church's bell, and this loudness and this harshness was such a surprise to the people who had ordered the cathedral and its clock and bell built and to the people who had built the cathedral and its clock and bell that these two peoples agreed to call the harsh loudness a chime and the chiming of the church bells marking off time eventually became a part of the great and everlasting silence. And Mr. Potter did not move with great hurry or inexorably toward his inevitable end, it was only that the end is so inevitable, his end was beyond avoidance, and yet like the hours trapped in a clock—let it be the clock on the top of the cathedral with its four faces, each facing a corner of the earth—the end of each hour is the beginning of the next, his end has a beginning and it rests in the small girls, each of them with his nose, and one of them can read and can write and perhaps this one shall remove him from the great and everlasting silence.

And: "Won't you come into my parlor," said the spider to the fly. Mr. Potter was remembering that someone had tried to help him recite the rest of that nursery rhyme, it was a nursery rhyme, that is what it was, something meant for children, and Mr. Potter thought, A child! But he was never a child, he had always been Mr. Potter (he said, "Me name Drickie, you know, me ah tell you, me name Drickie"). Parlor! Spider! Fly! Tomorrow is the same as today, was a fundamental way of organizing the world to Mr. Potter. Tomorrow will hold good, bad, the same as today, whatever that should be, was a fundamental way of organizing the world to Dr. Weizenger. Tomorrow, tomorrow, said Mr. Shoul, but he fell out of Mr. Potter's consciousness altogether for he died suddenly and his funeral was a spectacle. The procession following the hearse bearing his coffin extended for a mile or so, most of them people to whom Mr. Shoul had sold yards of cloth, or aluminum pans or basins or cups, most of them people who felt Mr. Shoul had made their lives better, but he had not made their lives better, he was the medium through which they felt their lives were better, but their lives were the same, the same, the same, always the same, for life is that way: the same. And the red clay that bound itself to Mr. Shoul as he lay dead was indifferent to Damascus and the road that went toward it and the road that went away from it, and that same red clay of Antigua that encased Dr. Weizenger as he lay dead in it was very different in texture from ashes; and Dr. Weizenger had once been very close to becoming only ashes, all that would have remained of him—ashes. And Dr. Weizenger died also, but he did not have a long funeral procession, for his patients did not like him or love him, though he had made their lives better, he had made them well when they had been sick, and none of the people he made well mourned him when he died, they only remembered that he had told them he did not like the way they smelled and he did not like dirt under their fingernails and he did not like their hair and he did not like their very existence, for they were so vulnerable and yet they persisted; and how their persistence annoyed him. So vulnerable was Dr. Weizenger and he perished in the warm clay that was the opposite of ashes, for everything was the same yet everything repudiated sameness. Dr. Weizenger's wife died, and his nurse died too; his wife and his nurse were the same person and her existence in the world was so ordinary and so ordinary and so ordinary again, it does not thrive under observation. And Mr. Potter did not move hurriedly toward his own end.

When Mr. Potter died, his death coincided with a natural calamity. It rained and the rain fell out of the sky as if what was at first a gash widened and widened until there was no sky above, only an ocean emptying itself out, and its contents fell on Mr. Potter's death and on everyone who had an interest in his death. I had no interest in his death, his being alive had only recently become known to me. Mr. Potter died, he died again and again, and he also died only once, in that way all people do, just die, die, and die. He died. And the rain fell and fell and my father's body, for Mr. Potter was my father, lay in Mr. Barnes's funeral home, a home that was a house with no windows at all, only a door through which everyone entered, dead or alive. And Mr. Barnes was the true father of Mr. Potter's only son and that son did not attend Mr. Potter's funeral, his name was Louis and he lived in Canada then and he died in Canada eventually, and how helpless is everyone and everything in the face of this eventuality, death. And all his girl children (I was not there) gathered around him, all their noses the same in shape and color, and they looked at him and looked at him searching for a sign of recognition, but he could not give them any, for he was dead, and his nose no longer looked like theirs. He was anonymous, the way the dead are, anonymous, and only the living can make sense of the dead, the dead cannot make sense of any living thing. And Mr. Potter's daughters could not make any sense of him.

So doomed was Mr. Potter to be encased within his own self, with all his limitations, and all his boundaries had no borders; so doomed was he to liking his own gait, as he imagined himself walking toward and away from Mr. Shoul's garage; doomed to liking the noses of his girl children as they appeared before him, sometimes through his own seeking them out, sometimes when he did not wish to know of their existence in the first place; and Mr. Potter was always himself, he was always Mr. Potter, and when he died it rained for many days, by coincidence the rain came after years of drought, and the people gathered around his grave quarreled as his coffin was about to be lowered into the ground, as he was about to vanish from the earth forever and with him any hope, any evidence of his love. And they quarreled over his love, for they had nothing to show for it but their noses. And all through that day of his burial, the rain fell and fell with such ferocious constancy, as if the world from then on would be made up only of that, rain and rain and rain, and the water gathered up in the hole, six feet deep, that was to be Mr. Potter's grave, and it stayed there, waiting, as if it were the beginning of something, a new world, but it was only Mr. Potter's grave and his burial had to be postponed, for the gravediggers could not bail out all the water that had gathered in his grave before nightfall. The day into which Mr. Potter had died was so much the opposite of the day into which the sun was always in the middle of the sky; the sun was blotted out, blotted out by an eternal basin of rain, and that basin had, by accident, been inverted.

How sad never to hear again the sound of a mother hen chirping with satisfaction at the sight of an overly bloated worm which she knows will be nourishment for her baby chicks; how sad never again to see a rainbow gracing the arch of the sky in that space before the horizon begins and ends; how sad never again to see the gleaming mound that is the top of a woman's breast; never to look up and see a sky sealed blue and blue and blue again, and to know that blue signals the sky's opposition to moisture-bearing clouds; how sad never to hear your name called again; how sad never to look up again and see the face of someone you recognize, someone you love or thought you loved, someone really dear to you, or someone you know to be dear to you because her nose is shaped exactly like your own; how sad never again to see a winged mammal wending its way in the cool, dark night; how sad never to touch your own toes again as you remove your shoes from your feet; how sad never to clasp yourself in your own arms again out of a sense of desolation or loneliness or approval or pleasure or knowing the sheer nothingness of such a gesture; how sad never to be able to look up at the vast expanse of endless emptiness above and the seeming limit of the ground on which you stood ever again; how sad never to again see the sun turn red sometimes and disappear sometimes; how sad never again to touch another person spontaneously, without thought, without reason, without justification, and to expect a similar response, and how sad to find yourself disappointed, one way or the other, the other or one way; how sad never again to stand in the middle of nowhere and see the world in all its brightness and brimming over with possibilities innumerable heading toward you; how sad to know that you will be alive once and never so again, no matter how you rearrange your life and your very own self. "So, me ah wharn you, me ah tell you, eh, eh!" said Mr. Potter when he was still alive and not dead and helpless, lying all alone in his coffin, dressed up in garments suitable for burial, his naked body swathed in a brand-new white linen suit. But when he was dead, he said nothing at all, and sadness or its opposite could not come from him; sadness or its opposite might be attached to him, but Mr. Potter himself was dead and could experience no such thing, could not experience anything at all, for he was dead. And the world in its entirety and the individuals who contribute to its entirety are small and smaller yet again, and how sad, how sad, how very sad is life, for its glorious beginnings end and the end is always an occasion for sadness, no matter what anyone says.

Oh, and there is the thinning of hair on your head, and your skin losing its firm, taut texture, and the loss of the thick substance that held your limbs together, and events and events again and the time lapsed between these events, and the failing to recall all these events and even the times between them! Oh! Oh! And never again to see the faces of all those female people named Andrina and Elaine and Cynthia and Elfrida Robinson and Annie Victoria Richardson and someone named Emma and the flower called Marigold, and Rachelle and Etta and Esther and Roma and Joycelynne and Sylvie, and to wonder sometimes if they had any needs and then to dismiss the idea of them having needs and then just completely forget their existence: Oh, how sad, so sad! So sad to be removed from life, with all its clutter: like the many girls with the same-shaped noses; the arrival of Mr. Shoul, the appearance of Dr. Weizenger, diminished the presence of Mr. Shepherd; to hold the loving attention of many women at once, without letting any one of them become aware of the presence of the others. So sad to meet the unexpected love, grief, huge loss, grief again. Oh, how sad! So sad! Too sad!

And on the day of Mr. Potter's burial, it rained and rained. A spout opened up in the sky and poured its contents into his grave and that was enough, for no other source of water marked his death. No one cried to show sorrow over his death and no one was sorry that he had died, they were only sorry they had known him, or sorry they had loved him, for he left them nothing at all. He left his wealth, his house and a large bank account, to a distant relative who had migrated to an island so small that only the very poor or the very rich could afford to live on it and sometimes they are the same thing. Oh, to be rescued from the oblivion of death must be a cry each of us makes in the middle of the darkest of nights, but who can hear it, who can hear our voices? And when Mr. Potter died, I could read and by then I had become a writer, and so when I heard of his death, to hear it was the same as to read it, and I heard through reading, Mr. Potter is dead, my father is dead, and I recognized that a source from which I flowed had been stanched. It was my mother who told me that my father had died: she said, "Potter dead, 'e dead you know, me ah tell you, eh, eh, me ah tell you," and she said it in the same tone of voice as if she were describing a natural catastrophe, a hurricane or an earthquake, as if she were noting something common and everyday: the sun did not shine the day she had put the starched white clothes out to dry. And how amazed I was to hear my own mother, who was alive, tell me that my father had died, for he was dead, she had never told me of his being alive. And at that moment I could read and I could write and I wrote then only about my mother, trying to explain to myself her life and why it should make sense to me, for my own life as I lived it had become irrevocably (and yet impossible to do so) untethered from her life and that was a natural thing to have occurred.

And it was Tan-Tan, the man who dug Mr. Potter's grave, who told me of how he tried to bail the water out of Mr. Potter's grave and how futile was his effort and how, in resignation, he just stood there with the rain falling down on him and then into Mr. Potter's grave, and how while standing, he crossed one leg over the other to balance himself and he put his hands together and then laced his fingers into each other tightly, so tightly that it hurt, and he had to unlace his fingers and just let himself stand there, his hands at his side, his pitchfork leaning against his body, and how he watched Mr. Potter's relations fiercely quarreling with each other and his grave filling up with water and the sky never clearing to reveal the sun and Tan-Tan said that the dead did not bother him, for he knew them so well and he didn't care about the dead one way or the other, and how the dead were always wrapped up in coffins made of mahogany or pitch pine and how indifferent he was to them, and I did not say to him then that love made you indifferent, I only shook my head up and down, backward and forward, in agreement or disagreement, one way or the other, and even I did not know what I meant. And in the world of graveyards and burying, Tan-Tan sailed away, as if he were a ship whose port was always on the horizon and the horizon kept shifting, as horizons will, and he only remembered Mr. Potter and his funeral and the burial because I asked him, I was by then someone who wrote, I said, I said, I asked . . . and in response to my statements and my questions, Tan-Tan showed me, many years after the actual event, the place where Mr. Potter had been buried, but instead of the fat, upright mound that should have been his grave, he showed me a place in the ground that looked as if it had been built by ants, or as if it had been made by a child who had the privilege of play. What, I asked Tan-Tan, Tell me something, I said to Tan-Tan, What am I looking at? And Tan-Tan said that this burial spot was where Mr. Potter had been buried, and that even though it had no official marker, even though there was not a headstone, he could remember it anyway, for how over Mr. Potter's grave there had been such a commotion, so much contention regarding who was really entitled to weep at the sight of Mr. Potter's coffin or who was entitled to weep at the memory of Mr. Potter, and how the rain came down and filled the hole of Mr. Potter's grave and how he tried to bail the water out of the grave in vain, and how he had had to place the coffin on a bier and carry it to the dead house and leave it there for the night and how, early the next morning, after it had stopped raining, only he, Tan-Tan, and Mr. Tongue, who was the overseer of the graveyard, had lowered Mr. Potter's body, which lay inside a coffin, into the ground. And Tan-Tan noted to himself how easy it was to lower Mr. Potter into the ground, especially with the assistance of Mr. Tongue, how easy it was.

And to start again at the beginning: Mr. Potter's appearance in the world was a combination of sadness, joy, and a chasm of silent horror for his mother (Elfrida Robinson) and indifference to his father (Nathaniel Potter), who had so many children that none of them could matter at all; and to the world he was of no consequence at all, for the world is filled with many people and each of them is like a second in a minute and a minute is in an hour and an hour is in a day and a day is in a week and a week is in a month and a month is in a year and a year is in a century and a century is in a millennium and a millennium is in the world and the world eventually becomes a picture trapped in a four-sided frame. And Mr. Potter's birth was equal to the fraction of a moment that had already been divided and he moved slowly, slowly toward this moment of Tan-Tan bailing water from his grave and Mr. Tongue being called on for assistance to bail water from his grave, and in that way Mr. Tongue became a witness to something obscure and without significance, Mr. Potter's burial, and only because I am his daughter, for I have his nose, and because I learned how to read and how to write, only so is Mr. Potter's life known, his smallness becomes large, his anonymity is stripped away, his silence broken. Mr. Potter himself says nothing, nothing at all. How sad it is never to hear the sound of your own voice again and sadder still never to have had a voice to begin with.

Here again for the last time is Mr. Potter, so sweetly new, emerging from the warmth of his mother's womb, swathed in a thick film of bloody mucus, the cage of cartilage that was his lungs expanding into its natural and eventual form: open and then closed, like a door or a musical instrument of a certain kind; the first true smile to appear on his face because he recognized the face of his true mother, Elfrida Robinson; a distant thud, a distant rumble, all frightening to the small boy he had become, and no one to offer an explanation that this was universal to every individual life, change was always accompanied by a thud and rumble; and here is a dramatic curve in his life, more like a tiny stream of water ambling along without any known destination, and this likeness of a carelessly ambling stream without destination that is suddenly interrupted and forced into the strict order of a dam or a reservoir becomes the reality of Mr. Potter's life when, in the middle of his boyhood, his mother Elfrida walks into the sea and he never sees her again, not her face or any other part of her and not in a dream or any other situation imagined or real, he never sees her again and for the rest of his life he longs for her in some form, imagined or real, but never allows himself to know this. And here is Mr. Potter with the enforced wallowing in his childhood with the innocently cruel group of people, the family Shepherd, his father Nathaniel passing him by coincidence in an alley in the village of Table Hill Gordon without saying hello, without any sign of recognition whatsoever; and here is Mr. Potter meeting Mr. Shoul, who had so recently been disenfranchised from the Lebanon and the road which led to Damascus and back, and Dr. Weizenger and his wife May, passengers in his taxi (Mr. Shoul's car, it was then), whose presence remained vivid in Mr. Potter's mind and he could remember, up to the moment he died, Mr. Shoul and Dr. Weizenger more perfectly and more accurately than he could his mother Elfrida, who had walked into the sea, and his father Nathaniel, who had never acknowledged him at all. And at the moment he died, Mr. Potter did not remember the girl children, all of whom had noses that looked like his own nose, and certainly he could not remember the names of their mothers or even their faces and Mr. Potter died in the way of great men and in the way of ordinary men, for all men die in the same way, they just die, cannot breathe, will no longer get up and walk, they die, they are dead. Oh, hear the bells of the Anglican cathedral ring in the city of St. John's, on the island of Antigua, not because this is a symbol of Mr. Potter's end or beginning, just hear them ring and see them ring, for I tell you that they do ring and you can read the words: the bell of the church rang: and it rang on the day Mr. Potter was born and it rang throughout all the days of his life and it rang also on the day that he died and the bell rang, indifferent to Mr. Potter's coming and going, indifferent to whether his coming and going was in regard to Mr. Shoul's garage, Dr. Weizenger's arrival after he, Dr. Weizenger, had survived ten lifetimes of horror and then lived one lifetime of ordinary, everyday horror, which is to say that he climbed out of bed every morning of every day and he climbed back into it at the beginning of every night. See the flat feet of the boy Drickie cross-ing the yard, away from the stone heap, toward the gate and out into the street that led to Mr. Shepherd's home and Mr. Potter's mother, Elfrida Robinson, walking into the sea and never returning from it.

And Mr. Potter died, so simple a thing, he died and will never be heard from again, except through me, for I can read and I can write my own name, which includes his name also, Elaine Cynthia Potter, and like him and his own father before him, I have a line drawn through me, a line has been drawn through me.

And staring at the place where Mr. Potter was buried, in a grave not quite six feet deep, not quite six feet long, and not quite four feet wide, a mound so worn down that it looked as if it been built by ants, by then I was a middle-aged woman and I could also see my mother's grave. Her name was Annie Victoria Richardson and she did not have a line drawn through her, and for my whole life up to then, to see my mother dead was an event I was afraid I would never witness, I had waged a battle to see my own mother dead, and from time to time I was certain I would lose. I had never imagined standing on my father's grave for I did not know I had a father at all and that he had a name. My father's absence will forever hang over my present and my present, at any given moment, will echo his absence, but my own existence, as far as I can understand, modified him not at all. And Mr. Potter grew old and I remained a child and my mother remained my mother and these three things, my father, me, my mother, remain the same into eternity, remain the same now, which is a definition of eternity. And my father, Mr. Potter, lay dead and buried at my feet in his own grave and my mother's grave was a short distance from his and I, Elaine Cynthia Potter and Elaine Cynthia Potter Richardson, stood on the earth above them for some time, not forever and ever, only for a long time. And for a very long time after that. And it was my mother, who had left the house she shared with my father, Mr. Potter, when I was seven months in her womb, who had taught me how to read but did not then tell me that my father could not do so, or that her teaching me how to read, which led to me knowing how to write, was a dagger, so to speak, directed at Mr. Potter, for he lived his life deliberately ignorant of my existence, as if I were in a secret chamber separated from the rest of the world and the world would never know of me, or suspect that I was in the world. And I now say, "Mr. Potter," but as I say his name, I am reading it also, and so to say his name and to imagine his life at the same time makes him whole and complete, not singular and fragmented, and this is because he is dead and beyond reading and writing and beyond contesting my authority to render him in my own image. Hear the sound of my mother being in love with him and the rain pat-patting against the hard dry ground and the galvanized tin roof of the house which was just one room with some windows. Hear the sound of my mother's harsh words directed at Mr. Potter, expressing her own disappointments and frustrations, all of which were far removed from him, but at that time I was all furled up inside her womb, growing and growing until the time I was expelled. Hear the sound of my mother's wounds as she left the house she shared with Mr. Potter and hear the sound of Mr. Potter as he experienced my mother's treachery. Hear the sound of my birth and my father turning his back against my presence in the world. Hear the arrival of Mr. Shoul and Dr. Zoltan Weizenger in the world of Mr. Potter and their presence in the world Mr. Potter occupied came about because all they had ever known was completely shattered and then vanished and so they had to begin again, re-create their own selves, make something new, but they couldn't do that at all. Hear Mr. Potter wending himself through the maze of his life in complete innocence, without ever knowing how like everyone else he was and without recognizing how ordinary is the uniqueness of life as it appears in each individual. Hear Mr. Potter, who was my father; hear his children and hear the women who bore those children; hear the end of life itself rushing like a predictable wave in a known ocean to engulf Mr. Potter. Hear Mr. Potter dead and lying on a cold slab of something and then his body placed in a wooden box but the wooden box cannot be placed in its grave, for the grave has filled up with water. Hear the cry of his mourners, who on learning of the contents of his will were all disappointed; hear the cry of the gravediggers when they could not place Mr.

Potter, who lay inside his coffin, in his grave, for his grave was filled up with water. Hear Mr. Potter! See Mr. Potter! Touch Mr. Potter!

Mr. Potter was my father, my father's name was Mr. Potter.